7/15

P9-AFK-889

For Sabie, the original
Miss Cuchifrito.
And Toto, too.
I miss you both.

Acknowledgments

I have to give it up to the Jump at the Sun peeps here—Andrea Pinkney, Lisa Holton, and Ken Geist—for letting the Cheetah Girls run wild. Also, Anath Garber, the one person who helped me find my Cheetah Girl powers. And, Lita Richardson, the one person who now has my back in the jiggy jungle. Primo thanks to the cover girl Cheetahs: Arike, Brandi, Imani, Jeni, and Mia. And to all the Cheetah Girls around the globe: Get diggity with the growl power, baby!

Introduction

Once upon a rhyme, there were two beautiful, bubble-icious girls named Galleria and Chanel, who were the best of friends and the brightest wanna-be stars in all the land. One night, they looked up in the sky at all the real, glittering stars and dreamed of a place where they, too, could shine forever. Under the spell of the moonlight, they made a secret pact that they would find this place no matter how long it took, no matter how hard they had to try. Then they would travel all over the world and share their cheetah-licious songs and supa-dupa sparkles with everyone who crossed their paths.

But it wasn't until Galleria and Chanel banded together with three other girls and unleashed their growl power that they discovered the jiggy jungle: that magical, cheetah-licious place inside of every dangerous, scary, crowded city where dreams really do come true. The jiggy jungle is the only place where every cheetah has its day!

The Cheetah Girls Credo

To earn my spots and rightful place in the world, I solemnly swear to honor and uphold the Cheetah Girls oath:

🐾 Cheetah Girls don't litter, they glitter. I will help my family, friends, and other Cheetah Girls whenever they need my love, support, or a *really* big hug.

🐾 All Cheetah Girls are created equal, but we are not alike. We come in different sizes, shapes, and colors, and hail from different cultures. I will not judge others by the color of their spots, but by their character.

- A true Cheetah Girl doesn't spend more time doing her hair than her homework. Hair extensions may be career extensions, but talent and skills will pay my bills.

- True Cheetah Girls can achieve without a weave—or a wiggle, jiggle, or a giggle. I promise to rely (mostly) on my brains, heart, and courage to reach my cheetah-licious potential!

- A brave Cheetah Girl isn't afraid to admit when she's scared. I promise to get on my knees and summon the growl power of the Cheetah Girls who came before me—including my mom, grandmoms, and the Supremes—and ask them to help me be strong.

- All Cheetah Girls make mistakes. I promise to admit when I'm wrong and will work to make it right. I'll also say I'm sorry, even when I don't want to.

- Grown-ups are not always right, but they are bigger, older, and louder. I will treat my teachers, parents, and people of authority with respect—and expect them to do the same!

🐾 True Cheetah Girls don't run with wolves or hang with hyenas. True Cheetahs pick much better friends. I will not try to get other people's approval by acting like a copycat.

🐾 To become the Cheetah Girl that only I can be, I promise not to follow anyone else's dreams but my own. No matter how much I quiver, shake, shiver, and quake!

🐾 Cheetah Girls were born for adventure. I promise to learn a language other than my own and travel around the world to meet my fellow Cheetah Girls.

Chapter 1

Toto must think my toes are dipped in Bark-B-Q sauce, the way he's trying to sneak a chomp-a-roni with his pointy fangs. I have just painted my toenails in a purply glitter shade called "Pow!" by S.N.A.P.S. Cosmetics and am lying on my bed with my feet dangling to the winds so they can dry.

"Guess what, big brother, you're gonna have to get your grub on somewhere else," I coo to the raggely pooch with dreadlocks whom I love more than life itself. "I, Galleria Garibaldi, supa divette-in-training, cannot afford to have Toto-tugged tootsies."

Mom isn't sure what breed Toto is, because she and Dad adopted him from the ASPCA before I was born. But when all the hair-sprayed ladies on the street stop and ask me, I say that he is a poodle instead of a "pastamuf-fin" (that's what I call him). It sounds more *hoity-toity*, and trust: that is a plus on the Upper East Side, where I live.

I stick the bottle of nail polish in my new cheetah backpack. I hold up my hands, and it looks like a thousand glittering stars are bounc-ing off my Pow!-painted tips. "Awright!" I tell myself. "This girlina-rina is gonna get herself noticed by first period, Toto. High school, at last!"

Tomorrow is my first day as a freshman at Fashion Industries High School, and I'm totally excited—and scared. I figure it can't hurt to make a big first impression—but painting my nails is also a way to get my mind off being so nervous.

I'm real glad Chuchie is coming over for din-ner tonight. That's Chanel Simmons to you—she's my partner-in-rhyme (aka Miss Cuchi-frito, Chanel No. 5, Miss Gigglebox, and about a gazillion other names I call her). We've known each other since we were in designer diapers. Chuchie, her brother, Pucci, and her mom, Juanita, ought to be here any minute, in fact.

Chuchie's going to Fashion Industries High, too. Thank gooseness—which is my way of saying thank you. She's about the only familiar face I'll be seeing come tomorrow morning.

Chanel is a blend of Dominican and Puerto Rican on her mother's side, Jamaican and Cuban on her father's side—and sneaky-deaky through and through! She lives down in Soho near my mother's store, Toto in New York . . . Fun in Diva Sizes. It's on West Broadway off Broome Street, where people are a lot more "freestyle" than in my neighborhood.

Down there, you can walk on the sidewalk next to a Park Avenue lady, or someone with blue hair, a nose ring, and a boom box getting their groove on walking down the sidewalk. Up here, hair colors must come out of a Clairol box. It's probably written in the lease!

"Galleria?" I hear my mom calling me from the dining room. "You 'bout ready, girlina? 'Cause your daddy's getting home late, and I'm not playing hostess with the mostest all by myself!"

"Coming, Momsy-poo!" I shout back. But I

3

don't move. Not yet. Plenty of time for that when the doorbell rings.

Thinking about Chanel has put me in mind of my music. I start singing the new song I have just finished writing in my Kitty Kat notebook: "Welcome to the Glitterdome."

I have to get my songs copyrighted so no one will bite my flavor before I become famous—which is going to happen any second. I have a drawer full of furry, spotted notebooks filled with all the words, songs, and crazy thoughts I think of—which I do on a 24-7 basis. I will whip out my notebook wherever I am and scribble madly. There is no shame in my game.

I pick up my private notebook, on which my name—Galleria—appears in peel-off glitter letters, and turn to a blank page. I start writing notes to myself and working on the "Glitterdome" song some more.

What I love the "bestesses of all" (as Chanel would say), is singing, rhyming, and blabbing my mouth. It's as natural to me as dressing for snaps (that means, for compliments). I can make up words and rhymes on a dime. Not rap, just freestyle flow. I also spell words "anyhoo I pleez"—as long as they're different from other people's spelling.

The doorbell rings. "Galleria!" my mom shouts. "You'd better wiggle you way over here. The 'royal' family has arrived!"

I slip into my cheetah ballet flats and hurry to get the door. Tonight's a big night for Chanel's mom, Juanita: She's introducing us to her new boyfriend. He's some kind of mysterious tycoon or something, whom she met in gay Paree, aka Paris, France, no less! From what Mom tells me, Juanita thinks he might be her ticket to the Billionaire's Ball, if there is such a thing.

"She met him in Paris, and he supposedly owns half of the continent or something," was how Mom put it. "She's trying to get him to marry her—so we've gotta make a good impression."

Well, okay. I guess I know how to make a good impression. Hope he likes purple glitter toenails, cause I am me, y'know? Like me or don't, I'm not fluttering my eyelashes like Cleopatra!

"Chuchie!" I say as I open the door. "Wuzup, *señorita*?" We do our secret handshake greeting, which consists of tickling each other's fingernails—and give each other a big hug.

Juanita looks like a glamapuss. Poly and Ester must have been on vacation. She's still as thin as she was when she was a model (unlike my mom, who is now a size-eighteen, class-A diva). Right now, Juanita's wearing this long, flowy dress encrusted with jewels, like she's the royal toast of gay Paree or something. Like I said, it looks good on her, but it's kinda weird if you ask me.

"Hey, Galleria!" she says. Then she steps sideways so I can see her new boyfriend. "This is Monsieur Tycoon," she says, laying on the French accent.

"Pleased to meet you," I say, offering my hand. But he doesn't take it. I guess over there they don't shake a girl's hand if they don't know her. "His Majesty" just smiles this teeny little smile and nods at me.

"Come on in, y'all," I say, and they do, Mr. Tycoon last of all. Juanita gives me a little wink as she passes and I can tell she's happy and nervous all at the same time. Pucci hugs my waist.

I look at Chuchie, and she rolls her eyes at me. I bite my lip to keep from giggling and wonder how Chuchie's managing not to giggle herself. She's always the first to lose it, not me. But that's because she's met the tycoon before.

He's good-lookin', all right, with a big black mustache and black eyes that make him look like he's an undercover spy. And he's wearing a pinstriped suit that's probably hand-sewn—every stitch of it! He comes in and looks around the place, nodding like he approves. I'm so glad he thinks we're worthy of his royal highness. *Not*. I mean, I am not used to being scrutinized, you know? I wonder how my mom is going to react.

"*Bon soir*," Mom says, flexing her French and gliding into the room from the kitchen, six feet tall and looking every inch the diva she is—still ferocious enough to pounce down any runway. The tycoon gives her a little bow and puts his hands together like he's praying, but I think it's because he's impressed.

"I hope you're all hungry," Mom says. "I've been in the kitchen all day, whipping up a *fabulous* feast."

I know she's fibbing, but I stay hush-hush. Mom *always* goes down to the Pink Tea Cup for dinner when she wants to serve soul food. Their stuff is greasy but yummy.

Me and Chanel give each other looks that say "We've gotta talk!"

"'Scuse us for a minute?" I ask the grown-ups. "I want to show Chanel my new cheetah backpack."

"Go on," Mom says. "We'll call you when dinner's served."

We hightail it into my room and shut the door behind us. As soon as we do, Chuchie explodes into a fit of giggles. "I can't take it anymore!" she gasps.

"Is he for real?" I ask. "Shhh! He'll hear you laughing and get insulted. You don't wanna mess things up for your mom!"

"She is so cuckoo for him!" Chuchie says.

"Chuchie, you're gonna be a royal princess one of these days, and I'm gonna have to bow down and throw petals at your corn-infested feet every time I see you."

"Stop!" Chuchie says again, dissolving into another fit of giggles. When she's finally done, she says, "Seriously, Bubbles. I'm worried about Mom. I mean, his 'Majesty' is so weird. I'm not even allowed to talk when he's around!

He thinks children are supposed to be seen and not heard." Chuchie calls me Bubbles because I chew so much bubble gum.

"Children?" I repeat. "Miss Cuchifrito, we're in high school come tomorrow! We are not children anymore!"

"Tell me about it! Are you ready for the big time?"

"Ready as I'll ever be—I've got my nails done (I flash them for her), my new backpack, and attitude to spare. How 'bout you, girlita?"

"I guess," she says, not sounding too sure of herself. "It's gonna be kinda strange not knowing anybody else but each other."

"Hey, we don't need anybody else," I tell her. "We are the dynamic duo, yo!"

Me and Chanel have been singing together since we were six, but not professionally, because Chanel's mom does not want her to be a singer. A talent show here or there is "cute," but after that she starts croaking.

What Juanita doesn't know is that me and Chuchie made a secret pact in seventh grade. We are going to be famous singers despite her (or maybe to spite her) because we can't be models like her and my mom were.

My mom is a whopper-stopper six feet tall. I'm only five feet four inches. Juanita is five feet seven inches. Chanel is five feet three inches. Do the math. We're both too short for the runway sashay. (My mom was a more successful and glam-glam model than Juanita—and sometimes I think that's why they fight.)

Unlike Juanita, my mom is pretty cool with whatever I'm down with. She wanted to be a singer really bad when she was young. She had the fiercest leopard clothes, but she just didn't have the voice. Then she went into modeling and sashayed till she parlayed her designing skills.

The only reason *I* haven't become a famous singer yet is because I don't want to be onstage by myself. Being an only child is lonely enough. I would go cuckoo for Cocoa Puffs, for sure. With Chuchie around, it's like having a sister. Like I said, we are the dynamic duo, bound till death. But, still, there's something missing—and I'm beginning to think I know what it is.

"You know what, Miss Cuchifrito?" I say. "I think we need to find us some backup singers and make a real girl group."

"Yeah!" she says right away. "Girl groups always become famous. Look at the Lollipops. They were finger-lickin' large."

"Or the HoneyDews," I say. "Their bank accounts are ripe with loot."

"Or Karma's Children, or The Spice Rack Girls!" Chuchie adds. "They are not even supa-chili anymore, but they once were, and that is what counts."

The kids in junior high school used to say that I look like Backstabba, the lead singer of Karma's Children. That is probably because I'm light-skinned (dark butterscotch-y) and wear my hair kinda long in straight or curly styles. (My hair is kinky, but I straighten it.) I don't think we look alike. I have bigger hips and tommyknockers (that means boobies). I also wear braces.

Karma's Children are four fly singers—Backstabba, Greedi, Peace, and Luvbug—from Houston and they must have instant karma because they had a hit record right out the box, "Yes, Yes, Yes." From what I can see, you don't have to have a lot of lyrics to be large. The Spice Rack Girls had a hit song with even fewer words—"Dance!"—and they live in a castle, I think, somewhere in Thyme City, Wales, which is far, far away from the jiggy jungle.

"Hey, if we get in a girl group, we could travel all over the world, singing," Chuchie says.

"We could go to London," I say, getting in the groove. "Drink Earl Grey tea with the queen."

"Yeah, and shop in the West End district." That's Chanel for you. Her idea of geography is knowing every shopping locale worldwide!

"We could go to Paris, too," I say. "Eat croissants with butter—not margarine!"

"Yeah, and shop at French designer saylons," Chuchie adds, stretching the long "a."

"Like Pouf," I say, "where they sell the *très* fiercest leopard-snakeskin boots. Then we can go to Italy to see all my aunts and uncles on my father's side."

"And shop at Prada! That's where I'm headed. 'Prada or Nada,' that's my motto for life!"

Chuchie picks up my hairbrush and starts singin' into it like it's a microphone—doin' Kahlua and Mo' Money Monique's "The Toyz Is Mine." I pick up my round brush and join her, both of us bouncin' on the bed as we sing and do our supa-dupa moves in perfect har-mo-nee.

Chanel kinda looks like a lighter version of Kahlua—with the same slanty, exotic brown eyes, and oodles of long micro-braids falling in her face.

When we're done, we both dissolve in giggles. Then I roll over and say, "We're gonna do it, Miss Cuchifrito. Alls we gotta do is find the rest of our girl group."

"Uh-huh. But where we gonna do that?" she asks me.

"I dunno," I say. "But one thing is for sure: It's gonna happen." We give each other our secret handshake and a fierce hug.

That's me and Chuchie: always hatchin' big dreams together. At first, we wanted to open a store for pampered pets—and now we have a game plan for becoming starlets. And you know what? One day, they're all gonna come true. Trust me.

"Hey! What are you two 'high school' girls doin' in there?" I hear Mom calling. "I got dindin on the table and I know you don't want cold pork chops and black-eyed peas!"

"Coming!" we both yell.

"I'll page you later," Chuchie says as we go to join the grown-ups. "We can 'dish and tell' later."

"You got it, girlita," I say. "'Cause I know I won't be able to sleep tonight. I'll log on when I get your page, and we can hog the chat room all night long."

Chapter 2

It's 10:45, and Chuchie, Pucci, Juanita, and Mr. Tycoon are long gone. Mom is cleaning up in the kitchen. My dad walked in about half an hour ago, and he's waving a piece of corn bread in the air as he talks. Talking with his hands comes with his heritage. Signore Francobollo Garibaldi is Eye-talian—from Bologna, Italy—but he loves soul food. I guess it comes with lovin' my mom.

Dad runs the factory in Brooklyn where the clothes are made for Mom's store, Toto in New York, and sometimes he gets home real late. Like tonight.

I give him a kiss, or *un bacio*, as he calls it, and say, "I got school tomorrow and I gotta get my beauty sleep, okay?"

"Okay, *cara*," my dad says, kissing me back. "Luv ya. Just make sure your skirt is longer than twelve inches!" He smiles at me and gives me a wink. *Cara* means "precious one" in Italian. That's my dad for you: behind me all the way, as long as I keep my knees covered!

I get washed up and get into bed, knowing Mom will be coming in to say good night any minute. She never misses. Sure enough there's a soft knock at my door, and she comes in and sits by my bed.

"You have a good time tonight?" she asks.

"Uh-huh. I guess," I say. "Mr. Tycoon's kinda different, though."

Mom laughs. "I know what you mean, sugah. You and Chanel didn't say two words the whole time, but I bet you were kicking each other under the table!" Mom knows us too well.

"Yeah." I giggled. "Better kicking than talking—I got the feeling he wouldn't like it if we did!"

"You're right about that," she says. "But Juanita's crazy 'bout him, so we've just gotta play along and hope she gets what she wants—and likes it when she does."

"Uh-huh," I say.

"You ready for school tomorrow? Just don't roll up the waistband of your skirt!" she says.

"Okay," I say, and fake a yawn. "G'night, Mom."

"Good night, baby. Don't be scared, now—stay fierce. Show 'em who you are, and they'll love you just like I do." She kisses me on the forehead and goes out, shutting the door behind her.

Mom is so cool. When I am rich and famous, I am going to buy her the one thing she wants more than anything else: Dorothy's ruby slippers from *The Wizard of Oz*. Mom is a *serious* collector. She wants whatever nobody else has, or almost nobody. There are only five pairs of ruby slippers in the whole world, and the last pair was auctioned off at Christie's for 165,000 duckets. I will find the anonymous mystery person who has bought the ruby slippers and buy them for Mom as a surprise.

Mom has seen *The Wizard of Oz* more times than I care to remember. She boo-hoos like a baby every time, too. I don't know why it makes her cry. It makes me laugh.

There is something Mom isn't telling me

about her family, but I'm not supposed to know that. She never talks about them, and I don't have any relatives on her side.

In the living room, there is a very old, gray-looking picture of *her* mom, a brown-skinned lady who looks sad. She says her mother died a long time ago, before I was born. Chanel says my mom is a drama queen. I think she is just larger than life. Diva size.

I have a lot of ruby slipper stickers, which I have put on my school notebooks and dresser drawers and my closet doors in my bedroom— the "spotted kingdom." I also have ruby slipper cards. I keep them in the leopard hat boxes by the bed.

Inside the ruby slipper card, it says MAY ALL YOUR DREAMS COME TRUE. I keep one pinned on my busybody board and open it sometimes because it gives me hope that my dreams will come true, too. I don't want to let my mother down and live in this bedroom forever.

My Miss Wiggy alarm clock reads 11:00, and suddenly, my beeper is vibrating on the nightstand. Got to be Chanel. I roll over, hop out of bed, and log on to the Internet on my swell Ladybug PC.

Toto is hunched on his front paws and staring at me with his little black beady eyes. My poor little brother can't accept the fact that he is simply a fluffy pooch. Toto is fifteen, (which is 105 in human years), and he sleeps in my room, in his very own canopy bed, with a leopard duvet. "Oh, Toto, you always make me smile," I tell him as I type my greeting to Chuchie.

"Chanel, Chanel, you're so swell. What are you wearing tomorrow, *mamacita*, pleez, pleez, tell?"

No answer. Hmmmm . . . she beeped me, but she isn't in the chat room. That's strange. There is plenty of cyber action, judging by the number of onscreen entries. Everybody must need a Net break since it's back to school "D-day" for anybody under eighteen with a brain.

"Oh, if I only had a brain, I wouldn't feel so lame, and I'd jump on the A train when it rained, because there'd be no shame in my game . . ." I hum aloud while plotting my next move.

"My name is Dorinda," flashes on my computer screen. "I'm pressing my khaki boot-cut pants right now and shining my Madd Monster shoes. I'm wearing a black sweater, right. Do you think it will be too 'that' to wear a tube top underneath it?"

Oh, this girl is mad funny, I think, cracking up as I type a response. "Hi, my name is Galleria. September is the time for the belly button to go on vacation and the brain to come back in full effect. Unless you want Serial Mom to corner you in the girls' room and cut off your top with a rusty pair of scissors, you'd better leave the 'boob tube' at home! Where are you going to school, anyway?"

"Galleria, the Joker, thanks. Tomorrow's my first day at Fashion Industries on Twenty-fourth Street. I'm going to major in fashion design! Guess I can't 'cut' class. Ha. Ha."

Hip-hop, hooray. This girl is going to the same school I am, even though our majors are different!

"I'm gonna be checking for you, girlita. I'm there tomorrow, too, or I'll be a T square. I'm majoring in fashion merchandising and buying—I've got a passion for fashion but can't cut my way out of Barbie's cardboard wardrobe. I leave that to my mom. She's a majordomo dope designer. You scared about going to high school?"

"No. I'm cooler than a fan, baby. Well, okey-dokey, a little," Dorinda replies. "It's farther away from my house than I'm used to traveling in the A.M., if you know what I'm saying. And it'll take away from the time I used to spend helping my mom get everyone ready for school."

Another entry flashes on my screen. "Hey, Bubbles! Let's wear our leopard miniskirts with berets, but with a different-colored turtleneck. Which do you want to wear, red or black?"

Chuchie is finally in the house. "Gucci for Chuchie! No diggity, no doubt. You're late. This is Dorinda and she's going to be in the house with us tomorrow. Where you been?"

"Pucci lost one of his Whacky Babies—Oscar the Ostrich. That beaten-up thing was his favorite, too. *Ay, caramba*, I was so glad that he finally fell asleep on top of Mr. Mushy. Now he'll be crying when he wakes up tomorrow and sees he's got a crushy Mr. Mushy, but I'm not moving him!"

Pucci is Chuchie's younger brother. He is nine, pudgy, spoiled to death, and has the biggest collection of Whacky Babies stuffed animals in the jungle. I call him "Eight

Ball" because his head is shaven clean like
a pool ball.

I type back, "Ooh, that's cold, Chanel No. 5.
Dorinda is majoring in fashion design. Ain't
that dope?"

"Cool, Miss Dorinda. Where do you live?"

"116th and Lenox Ave."

"Uptown, baby, you gets down, baby?"
Chuchie writes.

"I try. I can move. I can groove. I'm gonna
take dance classes at the YMCA on 135th 'cause
I'm in the Junior Youth Entrepreneur
Leadership Program there, so I get classes in
everything for free."

"We got skills, too. We take dance and voice
classes at Drinka Champagne's Conservatory
on Saturdays. You think you got more skills
than us?"

"No! I'm not flossin'."

"Correct, *mamacita*. Me and Galleria sing,
too. What you know about that?"

"Nothing. But I think I can sing, too—a little.
I would like to, anyway. I'll check for you two
tomorrow and show you!"

"Bet, Dorinda. Bubbles, don't try to get out of it.
What color top are you gonna wear? 'Cause you

better not wear the same color as me, *está bien?*"

"Bubbles? That's funny," Dorinda types.

"Chuchie calls me Bubbles because I love to chomp on gum. Something I cannot do in public because my mom says it's tick-tacky," I type for Dorinda. "I'll wear the red top with the black scribble, okay?" I type to ease Chuchie's mind.

"Dorinda, where did you go to junior high?"

"I went to Wagner," Dorinda types back.

"You really are a hoodie girl, huh?"

"Guess so. It was two blocks from my house. Easy breezy on the traveling tip."

"That's cool. It could be worse."

"Word?"

"Word. At least you don't live in the suburbs!" Chanel types, proud of her snaps. "Galleria is a boho because she is so 'that,' and I'm a Dominican bap, I guess, and proud of it. We'll see if you can hang with us!"

What does she mean by I'm so "that"? I'll fix her. "You're a burp!" I type back. "Boougie, undone, ridiculoso, and princess-y to the max. Don't deny it."

"Don't let me read you from cover to cover or you'll never recover, Secret Agent Bubbles, okay, *mija?*" responds Chanel. "I'm going to wear the black turtleneck top with the leopard skirt, so you can go ahead with your red top." I can just see her giggling. She is a majordomo gigglebox and can't be stopped.

"Maybe we can be a crew. You never know," I type for Dorinda's assurance.

"Let's meet outside the cafeteria at 12:00 sharp. But we're not going in. I don't want to get food poisoning my first day of school. You know what we'll be wearing, so you can't miss us!" Chanel signs off.

"See ya and I'm tryin' hard to be ya!" Dorinda retorts.

This girl is quick. Maybe she *can* hang with us, I think, as I sign off, "Powder to the People!"

"Powder to the People!" is a joke between me and Chanel. I'll tell Dorinda about it tomorrow. For now, I log off and get back into bed.

Toto is lying on the floor now with his nose pressed to the floor.

"Toto, watcha thinkin?" Cheez whiz, I wonder what it's like to be a dog. One thing is for sure. They don't have to get up at the crack of dawn and go to school.

In the darkness, my fears dance around like Lotto balls. So I sing out loud to all the twinkle-dinkles like me, trying to sparkle in this crazy place called the Big Apple. A real deal jungle. We don't have the grass and trees, but we do have some of the animals.

"Twinkle-dinkles, near or far,
stop the madness and be a star.

Take your seat on the Ferris wheel,
and strap yourself in for the man of steel.

Welcome to the Glitterdome.
It's any place you call home.

Give me props, I'll give you cash,
then show you where my sparkle's stashed.

Glitter, glitter. Don't be bitter!
Glitter, glitter. Don't be bitter!
Glitter, glitter. Don't be bitter!"

I drift into sleep, and I'm sure the fears have all been chased away. Not by my singing, but by Toto's snoring, which is louder than the backfire from the Cockadoodle Donuts truck that passes by our street at four A.M. every morning. My songs are my secret weapon, though, for shooting straight to stardom. . . .

Chapter 3

Mr. Drezform, our new homeroom teacher, has trouble pronouncing my last name, like all the other teachers I've had since kindergarten. "Galleria Gareboodi?"

"Here!" I yell out, smiling and raising my hand in the air like I just don't care. "It's Galleria Gar-i-bald-i."

This boy in front of me turns around and heckles me. "Gar-i-booty!" he says, and laughs. Then *everyone* else in the class turns to look at me.

"*What?*" I ask, challenging him. "What's your name, yo?"

"Derek," he says, still smiling.

"Derek what?"

"Derek Hambone," he says. "The new brotha' in town—from Detroit."

"Derek *what?*" I ask. "Did you say Hambone?" Now the class is laughing at him, not me. "Hah! You'd best not be laughing. Your last name sure ain't no Happy Meal."

I snarl and squint my eyes. He turns away, busted. Now I'm looking at the back of his head, which has the letters "D U H" shaved into it. "Duh?" I say to Chanel, mouthing the words without sound. "What are we on— *Sesame Street?*"

Derek is featuring a red, blue, and white Johnny BeDown shirt with matching droopy jeans covered with logos like a roadrunner map. Johnny BeDown clothes aren't made by the Joker, if you know what I'm saying. You have to shell out serious duckets for them. They just *look* like the homeless catch of the day.

There are three things I hate. 1. Cock-a-roaches. 2. Math tests. 3. Wack-a-doodle clothes. The first I can't avoid unless I move out of New York City. The second two are *kinda* like roaches because they're everywhere.

I, Galleria Garibaldi, will never dress like everybody else. I write this in my freshman notebook using my purple pen. It's true that I get my animal instincts from my mom, but I have my own flavor, 'cause I'll wear cheetah prints in hot pink or lime green, and Mom sticks to the old-school ones.

I remember I was only four years old when she bought me my first furry leopard coat with a matching hat. My father nicknamed me Miss Leoparda because I wore that coat to pieces. I also had a stuffed leopard animal named Cheetah Kat, which I took with me everywhere. And Toto now has seven leopard coats, thanks to me.

As for Chuchie, her taste in fashion runs to berets. She is wearing one today, with her braids hanging down into her face.

"Gimme one of your pens," she groans. "Mine stopped working." Chuchie must own about fifty of these French pancakes (that's what I call them). The beret she is wearing today is black with a gold-braided edge. Her mom brought it back from Paris. Chuchie is sitting next to me, drawing silly faces in the margins of her notebook and giggling quietly.

Attendance is taking a long time, and my mind wanders to Dorinda. We're meeting her at noon, outside the cafeteria. I wonder what she'll be like. . . .

Mr. Drezform blows his nose, causing Chuchie to giggle real loud, and Derek Hambone turns around and grins at me, giving me a big wink. Heavens to Bootsy—Derek has a gold tooth in front!

Chuchie dissolves into giggles, and I give her a hard elbow to the ribs.

"Hey, Derek," I say, "what's with the haircut?"

"Oh, you mean the letters?" he asks, giving me his goofy, gold-tooth smile again.

"Yeah."

"It's my initials," he explains proudly. "Derek Ulysses Hambone."

I bite down hard on my lip to keep from losing it completely. "You know, Derek, it also stands for something else."

"It does?" he asks, clueless. "What?"

"Figure it out, *scemo*," I quip, using the Italian word for idiot.

"Okay, I will," he says. "And *shame* on you back—even though, you know, you are cute." Another goofy grin, and he turns away again.

Great. Just what I need on my first day in

high school: a fashion disaster with a geeky smile and a gold tooth who *likes me*.

I can tell it's only a matter of time till he asks me out. Someone call 911, please.

"It's time for *lonchando*," Chanel says as we wait outside the cafeteria for Dorinda.

"I've got an idea for our Kats and Kittys Halloween Bash," I tell Chuchie. The Kats and Kittys Klub, which we belong to, does all kinds of phat stuff, and me and Chanel had been talking about the Halloween Bash ever since the Fourth of July. "We should throw it at the Cheetah-Rama, where Mom goes dancing. What do you think?"

"*Está bien*. I forgot to tell you. I saw those girls from Houston on Sunday down in Soho."

"What girls?"

"'Member the twins who were at the Kats Fourth of July Bash? What were their names?"

"Oh, I don't know. You're the one who was talking to them," I say, feeling a twinge of jealousy. She's talking about those wanna-be singers who showed up and sang when nobody asked them to.

"Aquanette and Anginette Walker," I mumble.

Of course; I do remember, because I remember everything.

Despite my flinching, Chuchie adds, "They can sing. They said they're coming to the Kats meeting on Friday. They moved here to go to Laguardia Performing Arts High. That's where we shoulda went."

"We didn't go because you were too scared to audition, 'cause of your mother, remember?" I point out.

If Chanel didn't go, I wasn't going to audition by myself, but yeah, I'd wanted to go there, too. I wonder if the twins had to audition to get into Laguardia. Or maybe they had "connects." They sure had the nerve to floss by singing at the Fourth of July barbecue grill, with the mosquitoes flying in their hair.

"True. They can sing," I say.

"And they can eat, too. The one in the red top ate seven hot dogs," Chanel says with a grimace.

"Which one has the name like the hair spray?"

"I can't remember, but they both had on a lot of that," Chanel says, giggling. "I thought maybe the one in the red top and white shorts had a television antenna up in that hairdo, it was so high."

Dorinda waves as soon as she sees us. I see she has taken my advice and is wearing a black turtleneck top with the khaki boot-leg pants. "Hi!" she exclaims, all excited. "I'm really, really *hungry*."

She is so tiny and pretty. I mean munchkin tiny. She doesn't look like a freshman at all. (She looks about twelve years old. For true.) She is also about the same color as Chanel—kinda like mochachino—and her hair is corn-rowed in the front, then the rest is just freestyle curly. From what I can see, she doesn't have a weave, unless it's an *unbeweavable* one, as Mom would say. Mom can "spook a weave" from the other side of the tracks. And I don't mean the ones in the subway, hello.

"Oh, word, I get to feel even shorter now," says Dorinda, squeezing between me and Chanel. "And I'm wearing heels!"

"We're three shorties," giggles Chanel, trying to make Dorinda feel better. Dorinda is even shorter than us. I feel so much taller with her around. I could get used to this.

"Here comes Derek," I mumble under my

breath. "Don't look at him," I plead with Dorinda.

Derek dips down the hallway and smirks in our direction as he passes. "Hey, Cheetah Girl," he hisses, winking at me. "I'm workin' on that puzzle you gave me." Mercifully, he keeps going.

Dorinda doesn't miss a thing. "Who's that?" she asks, squinching up her little nosy nose.

"That's Derek Hambone from our homeroom class."

"He's got on enough letters to teach Daffy Duck the alphabet," Dorinda says, chuckling.

"You are funny." Chuchie giggles. "You should see the way Galleria was looking at Derek in homeroom."

"Oh, don't try it, *señorita*," I counter. "Duh!"

"*Cheetah Girl*—that's kinda cool. You two are definitely blowing up the spots." Dorinda chuckles, fingering my cheetah backpack and reading the metal letters on the straps. 'Toto in New York'? What's that?"

"It's my mom's boutique—Toto in New York . . . Fun in Diva Sizes—down in Soho," I say. I notice that her tapestry backpack with happy faces is fly, too.

"What street is it on?" she asks me.

"West Broadway, off Broome Street," I tell her. "My mom makes these and sells them in her store."

"Really?"

"Really. She's a dope designer. Nobody makes clothes in diva sizes like she does. See how fat his stomach is?" I add, patting my backpack's paunchy stomach, "and the straps are leather, not pleather, like they put on the cheesy backpacks they sell on Fourteenth Street."

"How do you know it's a he?" Dorinda asks, her slanty brown eyes getting even slantier. Definitely Cheetah material.

"'Cause he eats more." I laugh, stuffing my textile design book into his fat paunch, then zip it up.

Dorinda has intense eyes, which she now focuses on Chuchie's cheetah. "You got one, too, huh?"

Chuchie nods her head and grins. "Whatever Secret Agent Bubbles gets, I get."

"You wish, you bumbling bourgeois detective!"

Chuchie hits me with her backpack.

"Oh, that's the top you said you were gonna wear," Dorinda says, turning to me. "What's it say?"

"Powder to the People. Grace is on the case. Will is chill. Sean is a fawn. I'm Fierce, You're Fierce," I say, pointing all over my top. "Whatever supa-licious things we come up with. Me and Chanel marked up a lot of tops this summer and sold them at our lemonade stand."

Dorinda really looks impressed.

"People were loving them. Bubbles's mom made them in bigger sizes and sold them in her store, too," Chuchie chimes in, bragging about our designing bite.

"Diva sizes," I say, correcting Chuchie.

"*Lo siento, mija.* I'm sorry!"

"My mom says there are no large sizes, just sizes that are too small!" I explain.

"I want to do some," Dorinda says.

"You gotta use black fabric marker so it won't wash off in the washing machine. But you can't put it on synthetic fabrics like polyester," I explain to her. "You could write on that with a blowtorch and it would bounce off."

Dorinda giggles ferociously. "That's funny.

How long you two been best friends?" she asks.

"Oh, this dish rag? I've known her since we took our first baby steps together. Both our mothers were models back in the day," I explain.

"Were they, like, in *Essence* magazine?" Dorinda asks me.

"My mom was. But the only modeling Juanita ever did was for *Chirpy Cheapies* catalogs, and Chanel has a lifetime supply of those wack-a-doodle-do clothes to prove it." I giggle.

"Yes, my mother was the diva of the discount catalogs, I confess, but it paid the bills, and now I got skills, okay?" Chanel snaps her fingers in Z formation. "My mom just wrote a book," she tells Dorinda. "She went all over Europe and Japan to write about the history of Black models since back in the day."

"Really?" Dorinda is hugging her books to her chest as we walk outside, cross the street, and slip into Mikki D's.

"Uh-huh. It's called *They Shoot Models, Don't They?*" Chanel says. "Get it? Photographers take pictures of models with cameras."

"Word. I got it."

"I just wish she would hurry up and get the money for it so she could give me some," Chanel whines in her best Miss Piggy voice as she orders from the Mikki D's counter clerk.

Chuchie is a shopaholic waiting to happen. Even I know that. Even worse than me. Getting ready for high school has left us pretty busted, though.

"These twenty-five duckets a week ain't stretching very far at the S.N.A.P.S. counter," Chanel says with a sigh.

"They are definitely drizzle duckets."

"What's that mean?" Dorinda asks.

"It means, 'If it rains, we poor!'" I giggle. "Stick with us and you'll learn a lot of words."

"I want to be a writer, too," Dorinda says. "I read a lot. My mom says I should open a library so I won't have to go there all the time."

"You go just for fun?" Chuchie asks in disbelief.

"Yeah. I take out books all the time. You should see how many books I got under my bed!"

"Like what kind of books?"

"You know. *Sistah's Rules. Snap Attacks. I'm Fierce, You're Fierce.*" She giggles, making fun of us.

She is mad funny. I didn't want to ask

Dorinda how much allowance she gets, because that would be rude. Our moms pay the bills for our cell phones, beepers, bedroom phones, Internet service, blah, blah, blah, but there are still so many other things that we want but we just have to "cheese" for it.

Chanel, of course, is much nosier than I am. She will ask anybody, anything, anytime— while she bats her eyelashes and acts all cute. "How much do you get?" she asks Dorinda, biting into her hamburger.

"For what?" Dorinda responds.

"For allowance, *mamacita*."

"Oh, I don't really get allowance. But I work at the YMCA Junior Youth Entrepreneur Leadership Program three nights a week, so I make about twenty dollars. If I was sixteen, at least I could get my working papers. That's how I could make some real bank."

"What classes you taking?" I ask Dorinda, changing the subject. I don't want her to feel like she can't hang with us just because she doesn't have duckets. Me and Chanel aren't with that.

"Sketching. English composition. Textile design. Biology. Computers—I love that. I'm gonna learn new technology applications like cyber rerouting and building databases."

"Computer nerd. You go," Chuchie smirfs. I have to laugh. Chuchie only uses the computer to get on the Internet and do her homework, otherwise she could care less about it.

"At least I got the dance class I want," Dorinda continues. "Dunk the funk. That's the move. I've had enough modern for a while."

"I heard that, *señorita*. We're taking it, too! What period you got?"

"Seventh."

"We're in the same class! That's dope," Chuchie exclaims.

Suddenly I remember something. "Check out this song I wrote last night," I say excitedly. And then I sing it for them:

"Twinkle-dinkles, near or far,
stop the madness and be a star.

Take your seat on the Ferris wheel,
and strap yourself in for the man of steel.

Welcome to the Glitterdome.
It's any place you call home.

Give me props, I'll give you cash,
then show you where my sparkle's stashed.

Glitter, glitter. Don't be bitter!
Glitter, glitter. Don't be bitter!
Glitter, glitter. Don't be bitter!
There's no place like the Glitterdome!"

"I like it, Bubbles!" Chanel says, then starts harmonizing with me. "There's no place like the G-l-i-t-t-e-r-d-o-m-e."

She is always down for bringing on the noise. There is nothing we love doing more than singing together—and Chuchie is better at putting music and melody to words than I am.

"Glitter, glitter. Don't be bitter!" Dorinda suddenly belts out, hitting the notes higher than even Chanel does.

"You *can* sing, *mamacita*," Chanel coos.

Chanel is like my sister, but I didn't choose her. We were bound together by lots of Gerber baby food and our diva mothers. Dorinda is different. She is just *like* us, and we only just met her!

"You should come with us to Drinka Champagne's Conservatory on Saturday,"

Chanel says excitedly. "That's where we take vocal lessons."

"How much is it?" Dorinda asks nervously.

"No duckets involved, Do'," Chanel counters. "We're on special scholarship."

"Do'. I like that," I remark, pulling out my Kitty Kat notebook. "Do' Re Mi. That's your official nickname now."

"Okay." She giggles, then scrunches her munchkin shoulders up to her ears. "I'm Do' Re Mi. My sister is gonna like that."

"What's her name?"

"Twinkie. She's nine."

"Like my brother, Pucci. Maybe we can hook them up," Chanel heckles on the mischief tip.

Then she gets an idea. "Oh, Bubbles, you know what would really be dope? Bringing Do' Re Mi to the Kats and Kittys Klub!"

"What's that?" Do' Re Mi yuks.

"Me and Bubbles belong to this 'shee, shee, boojie, boojie, oui, oui' social club—'for empowering African American teens!' Chanel chimes in, imitating the Kats president. "Before, they let us come for free because our mothers were members. Now we have to pay membership fees, but we can go by ourselves—finally!"

"How much does it cost?" Dorinda asks.

Clearly, Dorinda is all about the ka-ching, ka-ching. She is so smart. I really like her.

"It's about six hundred dollars, or is it six hundred fifty dollars a year for us till we're eighteen?"

"I think it's six hundred fifty dollars now."

"But don't worry, Do' Re Mi. We got you covered. We want you to sing with us, right, Galleria?"

"Uh-huh," I say. Chuchie doesn't make a move without asking me first. That's my girl-ita! "We're getting together a girl group, like The Spice Rack Girls, only better."

Dorinda brightens. "Awright! Where we gonna sing?"

"I don't know. We'll figure it out," I say. "We were thinkin' of singin' at the Kats and Kittys Halloween Bash. My mom's already makin' us Halloween costumes, anyway. I bet I can get her to make one for you, too."

"What does *your* mother do?" Chuchie asks Dorinda on the nosy tip.

"Nothing," she answers nervously. "She stays at home."

"How many brothers and sisters you have?"

Chanel asks, fluttering her eyelashes. Nosy posy just won't quit.

"Ten," Dorinda says.

"That's a lot of kids!"

"I know. But they aren't really *her* kids. I mean, she's a foster mother—and she's our mother, just not our *real* mother."

For once, Chanel stopped batting her eyelashes.

"Really? Are they your 'real' sisters and brothers?"

"No, but she's nice, my foster mom. She lets me do what I want, as long as I help her and stuff."

"You gonna come with us Friday, right?" Chanel says, not waiting for an answer. "We're on the party committee and we get to help plan all of the events."

I can tell she really likes Do' Re Mi. She is acting like a big sister. Just the way she acts with Pucci, her little brother. I wonder where Do' Re Mi's real mother is.

"You know we're the Kats, not the Kittys, right?" I say to amuse Do' Re Mi, then do the handshake wiggle with Chanel.

"I heard that. What's that you two are

doing?" she asks, extending her hand, too.

"Do it like this," Chanel says, showing her. The three of us wiggle our fingertips together. "All right! We got growl power, yo!"

I can see it coming. Now that we've found Dorinda, all our dreams are gonna come true. All we need now is another backup singer or two, and we'll be ready to pounce.

Chapter 4

With seven dollars in my cheetah wallet until Monday, there is only one filling solution before the Kats and Kittys Klub meeting: the Pizza Pit on Eighty-fourth and Columbus. When we step to the cash register to pay, much to our dee-light, Do' Re Mi makes a donation into the collection plate. "I got it," she says, giving the clerk $7.85 for our pizza slices and Cokes. "You're definitely crew now," Chanel says, giggling to the ka-ching of the cash register. One thing about Dorinda: She is generous with her money, even though she's got to work for it herself. I've never known anybody like that before.

We walk to the back of the Pizza Pit so we

can sit away from all the mothers with road-runner kids. The last time we sat up front, one of them threw a Dino-saurus Whacky Baby right into Chanel's large cup of Coke and knocked it over.

Chanel is sitting facing the entrance. "Look who just walked in," she says, talking through her straw, then quickly adds, "Don't turn around yet!"

It's too late. I already have—just in time to catch the grand entrance of those fabulous Walker twins from Houston. They are about the same height and size, but one of the twins is a chocolate shade lighter than the other. You can tell they're not from New York. The lighter-skinned of the two has on a hot pink turtleneck with a navy blue skirt. The other one has on an orange coatdress with ivory on the side. They look sorta church-y—at Easter time.

"Heh, y'all. How y'all doin'?" one of them says. The twins are kinda friendly in a goofy sort of way, and their southern accents just sorta shout at ya, "Y'ALL, we in the house!"

"Wuzup? You two coming to the Kats meeting?" I ask them, knowing full well they ain't here for a lobster cookout.

"Yeah, we're going over there. What we talking about tonight?"

"It's time for general elections. And we have to begin planning our next event. Me and Chanel are on the party committee. What committee are you on?"

"Volunteer services. We wanna plan something for a Christmas drive at a church or a women's shelter."

"We're planning to throw a dope Halloween bash," I counter. "Y'all missed our Christmas party." All of a sudden, I notice that I am trying to talk like them.

"Is that right?" one of the twins asks with a smile. She has nice lips—what we call juicy lips. Her eyes are big, too, like Popeye's.

"What's your name?" Dorinda asks her.

"Y'all, forgive me. I'm Aquanette," exclaims the twin with the pink acrylic nail tips. Okay, pink acrylics tips means Aquanette, I tell myself so I don't forget who's who. I wonder if Aquanette puts the rhinestones on her Pee Wee Press-On Nails by herself.

"You belong to Kats, too?"

"No. I'm just visiting. I'm Dorinda. Dorinda Rogers."

"They got good slices?" Aquanette asks Dorinda. She can't help but notice how quickly Dorinda is eating her food.

"Don't ask me if they're good. I'm just hungry," Dorinda says, smiling at her. Dorinda is s-o-o nice to everybody.

"We'd better order. We'll be right back," Aquanette says.

Anginette, it turns out, is the more vocal one in the ordering department. "Can we get a slice with anchovies, extra pepperoni, mushrooms, and sausage?" she asks the counter guy.

Chanel giggles at me, looking down at her pizza and kicking my Gucci loafers under the table.

"Watch the Gucci, Chuchie! It's leather, not pleather—like yours!"

Recovering from her laugh attack, Dorinda politely says to Anginette, who has returned with two slices and a Coca Cola, "I hear you two can sing."

"Yes, ma'am. You, too?"

"Well, sorta. I haven't been in any talent shows or anything, like Galleria and Chanel, but they're gonna take me to Drink some Conservatory with them for vocal classes."

"You mean Drinka Champagne's," Chanel says, cutting in. "It's the bomb for vocal and dance classes."

"Dag on, they got everything in this town," Anginette says with a tinge of know-it-allness in her voice. "That's why we came up here to go to Laguardia, 'cause they have the best vocal department in the country."

My first thought is, okay, was that supposed to be a one-up, two-down? My second thought is, she'd better not come for me or I'll read her like the Bible.

"We wanna be backup singers in a group," Aqua explains earnestly, slurping up the cheese from her slice.

"Forgive my sister. She hasn't eaten in five years," giggles her unidentical half. "Actually, we came up here because there ain't enough room in Houston for Karma's Children *and* us!"

Aqua is definitely the funny one. Karma's Children still live in Houston even though they're now famous.

"How old is Backstabba now?" Aquanette asks Chanel.

"They try to say she's eighteen, but I heard she's just sixteen. They still have a tutor who travels with them on the road, so it must be true, 'cause she ain't finished high school."

"I like Jiggie Jim," Angie says. "That falsetto voice, all that screeching—'Aaaaah got to know where you stand, gi-r-r-l,'" she sings, then gasps, "it just gives me goose bumps!"

Hmm. Angie is quite theatrical once she gets her pepperoni quota. She sure isn't biting off her twin sister's flavor.

"Jiggie's groove is cool, even though his voice is a little too high for me, if you know what I'm saying," I counter, smirking, "and I personally am not into guys who wear black sunglasses—at night, thank you."

"I heard there's something wrong with his eyes," Chanel offers, trying not to smirk. "His left eye doesn't talk to his right one."

We all howl. Chuchie *loves* to invent fib-ero-nis.

"Are you Spanish?" Anginette asks Chanel, whom she obviously finds amusing.

"Dominican, *mamacita*, and proud of it," Chanel says.

"You can call her Miss Cuchifrito," I offer bit-ingly. "She's going to give out *piñatas* around midnight."

"One week of Spanish and you ready to do show-and-tell," gasps Chanel, batting her lashes at me. "You know what a *piñata* is?" she asks the twins.

"Nope," say Anginette and Aquanette like a chorus.

"They're animals made out of papier-mâché and glue, then stuffed inside with candy," Chuchie explains. "When you hit the *piñata*, all the candy falls out!"

"Oh! I know what they are," Angie says. "They have them in the Santa Maria Parade in Houston."

"Are you Spanish, too?" Aquanette asks Dorinda.

"Nope, I don't think so."

"Is that right? You are so pretty. Ain't she cute, Angie?"

"Thank you," Dorinda says matter-of-factly. "Actually, I don't know my family. I live in a foster home."

Oopsy doopsy. That should keep our Southern Princess of Extra Pepperoni chomping quietly for at least a few minutes.

"We came up here to live with our father," Anginette says, trying to rescue her sister from putting another *"piñata"* in her mouth. "Our mother is a district manager for Avon, so she travels all the time. Our father felt we weren't being properly supervised since they got dee-vorced."

Their mother is an Avon lady. No wonder they're so nice. I am not gonna tell them that I only like S.N.A.P.S. Cosmetics. They've probably never heard of it.

"What does your dad do?" Do' Re Mi asks them.

"He's the senior vice president of marketing at Avon. He was my mom's boss. That's why he moved up here. They got any hot sauce here?" Aquanette asks, turning to her sister.

"Nope," Anginette answers.

"Well, then, gimme yours," Aqua says.

Out of Anginette's purse comes a bottle of hot stuff. We all burst out laughing.

"So it's like that?"

"Y'all laugh, that's okay. If our mother saw us, she would start some drama," Aqua says, pouring the Hot Texie Mama sauce on her slice.

Okay, this is hee-larious.

"They don't have this in New York, girls, so you have to bear with us. We is homesick!"

"Our mom won't let us use hot sauce because it's not good for our vocal chords. Our father don't say nothing, though," Anginette says, waiting for the bottle to come back her way.

"I didn't know that. See, Bubbles, you eat all that hot stuff. I'm glad I don't," Chanel says, acting all mighty.

"We're not supposed to drink soda, either, but I love it," Aquanette adds, slurping her Coke.

"Chanel drinks enough soda to do Coke commercials," I counter. These girls don't even drink Diet Coke. "Is it bad for your voice, too?"

"Yup. Y'all sing in a choir?"

"No, but we go to Drinka Champagne's Conservatory on Saturdays, religiously. We take voice, dance, and theater."

"Y'all should come up to Hallelujah Tabernacle on One Hundred Thirty-fifth and Lenox. We sing in the junior choir on Sundays."

"Well, I'm usually getting my pedicure at that time," I say, giggling. Aquanette has on too much white lipstick. Against her brown skin, it looks like a neon sign, I think, as both Chanel *and* Do' Re Mi kick me under the table from opposite sides. I am gonna make both of them polish my Gucci loafers, I swear.

"What's y'all's range?" I ask, imitating that cute southern drawl. Okay, so I am jealous. They sing in a choir, which means they can raise the roof off Jack in the Box.

"Mezzo, mostly," offers Anginette.

"Mezzo, too," adds Aquanette. "The gospel stuff is cool, but we want to sing pop, R and B-style music."

"So do we," Chanel says, nodding her head.

"Well, let's sing together sometime. Y'all can come over to our house!" Aquanette screams. "What y'all doing tomorrow night?"

"Well, we sure aren't going to the movies, because the duckets have run out," I say with a sigh.

"Nah, y'all can't be as broke as us. We are more broke than a bad joke! We need to make some money, doing *something*."

Now she is speaking my language. "Last summer, me and Chanel sold lemonade right on Second Avenue and Ninety-sixth Street near the big Duckets 'R' Us Bank, and we made some serious bank. How much did we make last summer, Chanel?"

"Lemme see. About four hundred dollars.

We may have to dust off my Mom's Tiffany pitchers and set up shop again, I swear," she says, giggling.

All of a sudden, I get a brainstorm. "Hey, y'all—we should perform at the Kats and Kittys Halloween Bash. You know, like charge admission. There's five of us—shoot. We could put on a show, we'd be, like, The Black Spice Rack Girls! And wear costumes with, like, spice leaves hanging off or something. I'd pay five dollars to see that!"

"Five dollars? How 'bout twenty-five dollars?" says Do' Re Mi, egging us on.

"Oh, my G-O-D, girl, that's a good idea!" yells Aquanette.

"My mom can *make* our costumes," I offer, bragging about my designing mom once again. She is gonna kill me. No, she'll probably charge me. But I'll worry about that later. "Last year, over one thousand Kats and Kittys came to our Christmas party. And they came from all over the country."

Okay, so I am exaggerating. But they did come from New Jersey, Philadelphia, Connecticut, Westchester, and even D.C., aka Chocolate City. There are over a hundred Kats and Kittys chapters across the country, but New York is the dopest one, and we throw the "dopiest dope" parties. Everybody comes to jam with us.

I'm not sure yet if I like these girls, but I know a ka-ching when I see one. Me, Chanel, and Do' Re Mi have got the flavor, but these two have the voices, and together we can at least put on one show. But first, I know we better get a few things straight before we go blabbing before the committee.

All serious, I say to the twins, "We're gonna go in there and ask the board members to let us do this. How come the two of you don't want to sing by yourselves? What do you need us for?"

"Me and Angie aren't about drawing attention to ourselves. That's not how we were raised," Aqua says, moving her acrylic tips to her chest, then turning to look at her sister. It's crystal clear which of these two operates this choo-choo train.

"We sing in the church—that's one thing— but we're about being humble," Angie says, looking at me earnestly.

Then, like she's on the *True Confessions* talk show, Angie says, "I honestly don't think we are flashy enough to be in a group by ourselves."

I have to give it to them: There is more to these fabulous Walker twins than hot sauce, tips, and chedda waves. They seem serious. "So you think that the five of us together could do some serious damage?" I ask, smiling at Chanel and Do' Re Mi.

"I think we should try it. If it don't work out, at least we'll have had a little fun with the show, then split the money and keep on searching for the rainbow," Angie says, fingering her arts-and-craftsy earrings.

Do' Re Mi steps to the home run plate. "We'll have to agree on the costumes and stuff, because we are not gospel kinda girls."

"We know that. We can see!" Aqua claims. "You three have that New York style. We are not going to come into this and take over. We *want* to be in a group."

"Okeydokey, then. The committee will go for it, right, Chuchie?"

Chuchie nods her head yes.

"All right, then," I say. "It's time to get busy in the jiggy jungle—no diggity, no doubt."

Chapter 5

*C*hanel and her family, Pucci and Juanita, live in a cheetah-certified loft on Mercer Street in Soho. (Yes, Mom helped decorate it.) In one part of the loft, Juanita has built a dance-exercise studio completely surrounded by mirrors. She likes to look in the mirror when she's exercising, which she does a lot.

Today she is in the studio giving herself exotic dance lessons and listening to some music that sounds *très exotique*. Maybe Juanita thinks moving her middle will make her a riddle to Mr. Tycoon.

"Hi, Galleria," Juanita calls out to me when I peek into the loft. Juanita hasn't gained an ounce since her modeling days. She brags about it all the time. Today she has on a crop top, and a sarong (like you wear at the beach) wrapped around her waist. She is moving a leopard scarf in front of her face right below her eyes, like she thinks she's the Queen of mystery.

"You girls want to come in here?" she asks me without missing a beat.

"No, we're going into the den," I yell back, trying to keep a straight face. Juanita thinks it's cute that we are performing at the Kats show. She has been in a very good mood lately, thanks to Mr. Tycoon.

The way she is wiggling her hips is too much for me. I run into Chuchie's bedroom and start wiggling my hips with my hands over my head. "I know, *mami*," Chuchie says, giggling, then rolling her eyes to the ceiling.

We have been rehearsing for a week, and everybody is getting on everybody's nerves. We can't seem to agree on what music to play for the show, but now it's show time—or, I should say, a showdown. Aqua and Angie are already waiting in the den with the records they want to use for the show.

Me and Chuchie walk into the den prepared to battle. See, our music tastes are exactly the same. We both like Kahlua, and we both like my songs—simple! Right now, I'm ready to throw down for my songs, and I must figure out how to get my way.

Do' Re Mi is sitting there quietly, reading a book called *The Shoe Business Must Go On*. She's very into shoes lately—especially the kind that make her taller! And, of course, she's always into books. I guess that's why she's so smart. Well, I hope she's smart enough to be on my side now.

"Okay, y'all," I begin. "We gotta figure out what we're gonna sing at the bash."

"I love Prince," Chuchie says, starting the negotiations. "Can we do his song 'Raspberry Beret'?"

"No," I say without even thinking. I can't believe her! I mean, what is she thinking? And didn't I just get through saying our tastes were the same in music? Yaaa!!!

"Who gets to choose the music, anyway?" Do' Re Mi asks, getting right to the point.

"We all do, but can't we pick songs by girls?" I say, stumbling. This is not going well. I need a mochachino.

"Who do y'all like?" Chuchie asks Aqua, imitating the twins' accent.

Aquanette says, "I told you. Karma's Children, Jiggie, Ophelia—"

"Uh-uh. No gospel!" Do' Re Mi says, sucking her teeth.

"I brought some house records from my mom," I say. "They're tracks without lyrics, so it will be easy to put my music to them."

There. I've slipped it in. Let's see if anybody has any objections.

"What do you mean, *your* music?" Aqua counters.

Dag on! I think to myself, imitating her. Why can't she just accept that I'm the leader of this pack?

"The songs I write," I explain patiently, pulling out my Kitty Kat notebook. "Don't act like you haven't seen this. I'm writing in it all the time!"

"Oh, *those* songs," Angie says, snuffing me.

So it's like that. I realize I'd better be quiet, before I go off. I guess it's my own fault. What with all the excitement about formin' a group, I hadn't mentioned to them that we would be performing *my* songs, too.

On the other hand, what's wrong with sin-gin' my songs? What do they think we're gonna sing: "Amazing Grace"? See, I'm 'bout to go off, so I'd better shut up for a change.

"What about that group, the Divas?" Angie says, trying to be the peacemaker. "Why can't we do one of their songs, like 'I'll Crush You Like a Broken Record' or 'I Will Defy'?"

It turns out that Angie and Aqua only like gospel singers. I say, "Good as we are, we aren't good enough singers to pull *that* off."

I knew I shouldn't have flapped my lips. I can see them looking at me like, what's she all mad about?

"Me and Chuchie like girl-group types of songs," I say, moving on to another point. "Do' Re Mi is partial to rap—plain and simple."

"Okay, what about 'Nothing But a Pound Cake'?" Aqua asks. This is her idea of compromise? That song is by Sista Fudge, who is a powerhouse singer. She *can* raise the roof off Jack in the Box.

"Aqua, can you just get it into your head that the rest of us can't carry a song like that? We don't have the vocal range!" I scream at her. "And can you pleez think about something else besides eating, okay?"

Oops, I went and restarted the Civil War. Aqua gives me a look that shoots right through me.

"Yeah, that's right. We're so used to singing together or with the choir, I forget y'all can't sing like us," she says, showing off, no doubt. "We definitely need to pick pop songs so y'all can stay in the middle notes."

After two hours of fighting, we finally pick two songs we can all agree on.

The singer we *all* like is Kahlua. We choose two of her songs: "Don't Lox Me out the Box," and "The Toyz Is Mine," which is a duet Kahlua does with Mo' Money Monique. It actually is perfect for five-part harmony because it has lots of choruses and refrains.

Of course, I still want to add some of my own songs to the mix. What is wrong with Aqua? I ought to clock her. And Angie, too. She is more sneaky. She'll smile in your face, then go along with her sister. First thing I'll do is drill right into Angie's chedda waves!

I can't deal with this drama today, not until I talk with Mom and figure out how to tell Aqua and Angie (without going off) that we are singing at least *one* of my songs. I know we are only doing this for a Halloween show, but it would make it so much more fun.

Forming the group (at least for the bash) has inspired me to write a song about it called "Wanna-be Stars in the Jiggy Jungle." I've been dying to let them hear it for days now.

Well, later for them. I know my songs are dope. They are probably jealous. They can sing, but they can't write songs. Angie and Aqua already told us that. They are gonna have to give it up.

"Okay, girls. Time to go home! I'm expecting company, and I don't want a bunch of kids hangin' round when he gets here," Juanita yells. Chuchie and me look at each other and stifle a giggle. We know who "he" is, all right. Juanita and Mr. Tycoon are doing the tango. Pretty soon, she's gonna be showin' off the rock—and is it ever gonna be a boulder! It'll probably topple her over.

"I have to go, anyway," Do' Re Mi says. "I've gotta go baby-sit my brothers and sisters while my mom takes one of the kids down to the foster care agency."

"Why, wuzup?" Juanita asks. "Is everything okay at home, baby?"

"Um . . . uh-huh," Dorinda says, pasting a

smile on her face. But I know, and so do Chuchie and Juanita, that things at Do' Re Mi's house are always in crisis. Kids comin', kids goin', all the time. I feel bad for her. It really makes me and Chuchie appreciate all we've got: two parents who love us (even though Chuchie's are divorced), and plenty of duckets for whatever we need (even if we do have to do a lot of cheesin' to get it).

I'm glad we got Do' Re Mi into our girl group. Once we perform, we're gonna get her into the Kats and Kittys for free. We already arranged to get her into Drinka Champagne's for nothing—Drinka calls it a "scholarship." Well, Do' is sure a scholar.

"Bye, Miss Simmons," I hear Angie and Aqua yell to Juanita.

Now that the others have gone, me and Chuchie have to go look at a few spaces. As the officers on the party committee, it's our job to find a club to hold the event.

We need to find a majordomo club, too, because a lot of Kats and Kittys will come to a party as laced as this one. Mrs. Bugge, the club president, will then work out an arrangement with the club owner after we choose a space.

That's the one thing I like about being an officer at the Kats and Kittys Klub: We get to feel large and in charge—even though we are "minors." (Yuk. I hate that word.)

"Let's check out the Cheetah-Rama," I say to Chanel, who is lost in her own *Telemundo* channel. I can tell there is something on Chanel's mind because she is real quiet, and Chuchie is not a quiet girlita, if you follow the bouncing ball.

Chanel leans on the refrigerator door, twirling one of her braids for a second, then takes a deep breath and blurts out, "Who's gonna be the lead singer of the group?"

"Me and you, *of course*," I answer, trying to be chill. "Look, Do' is the best dancer. No doubt. She can harmonize with us. Aqua and Angie are the background singers. That's cool, right?"

"*Está bien, mamacita*." She breaks out into a smile. I know she wants to sing lead on "The Toyz Is Mine." And that's fine by me, 'cause when we sing *my* songs—and we *are* gonna sing my songs—there's only gonna be one lead singer: and that's me.

Chapter 6

Seventh period, every Thursday, dance class is definitely the highlight of our week. Me, Chanel, and Do' Re Mi are a crew now. We meet during lunch and after school every day. Then we go over to Chanel's loft in Soho and practice our vocals with Aqua and Angie. (Things are still touchy between us, but I'm not touching it—for now.)

Today, I'm wearing a calfskin black blazer with a matching miniskirt and a cheetah-print turtleneck. Chanel has on leopard jeans and a red top. Do' Re Mi is wearing a black denim jumper. She has it zipped down a little so you can see her red tank top.

I want to surprise Do' Re Mi with a cheetah

backpack when we go to my mom's boutique on Saturday, so I've been really nice for a change. I've helped clean the kitchen every night and I've been reorganizing my room.

Last night, me and my mom watched a special on chimpanzees as we hand-sewed some new leopard pillow shams for the bedrooms. Dad says the best tailors in Italy still sew by hand, and he said he was proud of me. When we got ready for bed, I rubbed Mom's shoulders. She told me to stop tickling her. I'll get better at it. I'm sure Do' has a book I could read on massage.

In the locker room, Dorinda takes off her top. She always wears a white training bra, but she doesn't have much to train. She is flat-chested like Chanel. Ouch. I don't know if it bothers Do' Re Mi, so I don't have jokes about that. I wear a regular 34B bra already, and I've got the big hips to go with it.

Do' Re Mi hums to herself all the time, now that we are singers. She is so tiny, she easily could have been a ballerina. She has a perfect little body. She is really muscular.

"I took gymnastics all through junior high," Do' Re Mi tells us while she is changing. "I miss it."

"You have to have perfect balance for that, right?" Chuchie asks.

"No doubt," explains Do' Re Mi. "That horse is no joke. Once I came down hard on it. I was about six—and bam! I hit my thigh. I was crying. Mrs. Bosco—I mean my mother—had to come to school to take me home."

Mrs. Bosco. That is the name of her foster mother, I realize. Do' Re Mi never told us that before. I wonder if the kids in school ever made fun of her for having a foster mother instead of a real mom.

"Did you tell your mother about the show we're doing?" Chuchie asks her.

"Of course, silly. She says it's cool," Do' Re Mi explains, stuffing her clothes in a locker. "But she really wants me to be a teacher. I don't want to do that."

I wonder where Do' Re Mi's real mother is, but I'm not going to ask her that. I hope one day she will tell us.

"Where did you get your, um, last name from?" Dorinda asks me, hesitating. "It's so different."

"My dad is Eye-talian." I giggle. "He's from Bologna, Italy. There was a guy named

Garibaldi in Italy. He was a hero because he freed the country."

I change into the new leopard bodysuit I just got that I'm going to wear with black tights. "My dad says he saw his first opera when he was nine," I tell Do' Re Mi, because she is very into me talking about my family, anyway. "It had a Black opera diva from the United States, and that's when he knew he would come to the United States."

I wonder if my dad's dreams have come true. He says he wanted to marry a Black opera diva, but that Mom is the closest thing because she looks like one. When they joke around, she mouths opera for him, and he sits in the chair and watches her. I try not to laugh.

Me and Chanel like to stay in the back of the gymnasium, just in case we feel like doing different dance steps or making up new moves. Dorinda likes to stay in the front. She is the best dancer in the class, and Ms. Pidgenfeat smiles at her as she walks around to correct our movements.

"Everybody watch Dorinda," she yells whenever she wants us to get a dance step down. Do' Re Mi has all the moves down to jiggy perfection. I'm kinda jealous, but then I think about how much I like her. She is definitely crew forever.

Today we go back to Drinka Champagne's Conservatory for our vocal lessons. They were closed for a very long summer vacation because Drinka was on tour in Japan. She is a famous singer from the disco era, who founded the conservatory for divettes-in-training like me and Chanel. (After practicing with Aqua and Angie, I do realize how much practice *I* need.)

Drinka had an ultra-hit disco song back in the day called "Just Sippin' When I'm Not Tippin'." It was number one on the Billboard Dance Charts in 1972 for thirty-seven weeks. I know this because she has told us about the same number of times.

Drinka is finishing a class and standing by the receptionist. She is wearing silver spandex pants with a matching top, and a silver apple-jack hat that almost covers her face. Her pointy sequined slippers (yes, they're silver) curl up at the toes and make her look like Tinker Bell. "I think it looks like she's got tinfoil on her feet!" argues Do' Re Mi.

Everyone at the conservatory is excited about our singing at the Kats and Kittys Halloween Bash.

"Get paid, girls!" Miss Winnie, the receptionist, says, cheering us on. She is so nice. "You girls are gonna have to work hard together," she explains, giving Do' Re Mi her very own card stamped VOCAL 201. Do' Re Mi is supposed to start with Beginners Vocal 101, but because we're performing together, Miss Winnie lets her join our class.

For the first thirty minutes of class, we do scales. Wolfman Lupe plays the piano to guide our vocal warm-up. Doing scales means singing from the upper to the lower chambers in the voice to help loosen it up. It's kinda like stretching before dancing.

After warm-up, Drinka comes into the studio and teaches the vocal class. "Okay, pretty girls, show me what you can do," Drinka says, clapping. She tells us, "You have got to have a theme and a dream and a mind like a money machine."

We are lucky, no doubt, to be getting such primo vocal training for free. For the past two years, we've also gotten to take dance classes here, too. I mean we've learned all the global moves. Caribbean, Brazilian, and African are my favorite dance classes because we get to stomp around to the beat of live drummers. In salsa class, we dance to musicians playing conga drums.

After Drinka's, we have to hook up with Angie and Aqua at the subway station. I call them on my cell phone to make sure they're on the way. Angie and Aqua are coming from Ninety-sixth Street and Riverside Drive, where they live with their father. We meet them at the end of the platform at the Times Square station.

We have to take the N train to the Prince Street station to go to my mom's boutique. Aqua, Angie, and Do' (Do' Re Mi's shortened nickname) sit huddled together on one subway seat while me and Chuchie sit on a parallel one. I think the three of them—Angie, Aqua, and Do' Re Mi—feel more relaxed together, even though we are *all* a crew. I mean, Do' Re Mi loves to cook and sew, and so do Angie and Aqua. They all cook at home, too. They're huddled together peeping at a recipe for "Dumbo Gumbo" in *Sistarella* magazine. Like me, Chuchie is not interested in cooking. It takes her an hour to boil Minute rice. (She cooked it once. Yuk.)

The officers of the Kats and Kittys Klub were excited about our upcoming performance at the Halloween bash. "Why didn't you two think of this before, Galleria?" asked Ms. Bugge, when we told her our plans.

I told her, "Me and Chanel never wanted to perform by ourselves. That's not our idea of a show."

Now there are five of us. Five fab divettes. Hmmm . . . maybe that would be a good name for the group. . . .

I pull out my Kitty Kat notebook and start to dawdle and diddle. Five Fab Divettes. Nah. It sounds like a set of dining room chairs.

See, you have to have a catchy name for a group, and a theme that comes from the heart. That's what Drinka was tryin' to tell us.

Do' Re Mi looks at us and asks if everything is okeydokey. She is always looking out for her peeps. I like that about her.

"We're chillin'." I smile. "You like house music?"

"Some of it," Do' Re Mi says, shrugging. "Why?"

"We can borrow some of my mom's records to use as tracks for the show." Now that we have memorized the lyrics to both of Kahlua's songs (a small miracle), we can concentrate on my songs. And my songs need tracks. That's where my mom's house music comes in. All music, no words. Angie and Aqua still haven't given in on singing my songs, so I expect another battle on this. But I figure if I have Do' Re Mi on my side, that will make three against two.

"Sometimes my mom cranks up the house music in the store and dances. She says it's like going to church," I tell her.

"That's funny." Aqua laughs, hearing me. "She should come to our church. She'd have a good time, then. 'Cause we get down."

We are planning a trip to Aqua and Angie's church, but not until after the show, because we are all mad hectic. I pray that Aqua and Angie don't suggest we use gospel music tracks for the show. For now, it's too noisy to talk about it. That's the subway for you.

We are going down to my mom's store to see if she will make our costumes. Of course, I know my mom will make me sign an IOU—

which really means, pay now *and* pay later. Pay later in duckets, and pay now by cleaning my room. Not every day, mind you, but every hour.

I also want to give Do', Aqua, and Angie a surprise. The question is, will my mom cough up three more cheetah backpacks so we can look like a real crew? (Stay tuned, Kats and Kittys, to find out. . . .)

My mom's boutique is the brightest store on the block. You can see it all the way down West Broadway, which is a five-block-long strip of boutiques. A lot of famous divas come to my mother's store to shop.

We climb the five steps up to the big glass door entrance of Toto in New York. "If my mom offers you anything to eat, take it or she'll think there's something wrong with you," I whisper to Do' Re Mi.

Chanel presses the buzzer so we can get buzzed in. All the dope boutiques in New York have buzzers because a lot of shop-lifters, or boosters, try to come in and "mop" stuff. That means shopping for free. Boosters don't usually come into my mother's store because they are more scared of her than of the police.

"Ooh, Toto in New York, that is so cute," Angie says, looking up at the lime green and hot pink sign flapping in the wind.

"Ooh, look at all the leopard clothes. They got clothes to fit us?" Aqua asks all excited when we get inside.

"You keep eating like you do and they will," I smirk as we plop down on the big leopard-print love seat and wait for my mom. We can't interrupt her because she is doing her leg lifts against the counter. A house music song, "You Think You're Fierce," is playing on the sound system.

"See, that's house music," I mumble to Aqua. Bet they've never met anyone like my mother in Texas. Aqua and Angie are watching my mother in awe. (Their mouths are open.)

Mom weighs 250 pounds. That's 120 pounds more than she did as a model—something "Madame" Simmons loves to make digs about—but she is as beautiful now as she was back then. And I'm not saying this because she is my mother. My mom was and is a real diva—not just "back in the day," but today.

"We can't walk down the streets without some man goospitating and whistling at her," I tell Do' Re Mi proudly. "One guy stopped us right and asked my mom, "Girl, is it your birthday, 'cause you sure got a lot of cakes back there?" She hit that bumbling Bozo over the head with her leopard pocketbook. "I'm sure he's still recovering, somewhere over the rainbow." I smirk at Do' Re Mi.

Get me through this show, I pray silently to Mom's Josephine Baker poster. (See, an old-school diva like Baker, who used to have a leopard for a pet, understands what I'm going through.)

"Where's Toto?" I ask.

"Toto, come here, cream puff. I said come here!" Mom screams. Poor Toto comes charging out of the dressing room, where he was sleeping on the cushion, and makes a beeline under the couch because he doesn't see me. His hair is matted on the side like mine is when I first get up in the morning.

"Galleria, look at Toto! He gets so scared when I yell at him—he looks like a dancing mop!" Mom screeches.

"Come here, Toto. I want you to meet my

friends," I coo, trying to comb out Toto's hair with my fingers. I like when his hair is perfect like cotton candy, but Mom likes the untamed look, so he only goes to the beauty parlor every two months. Toto is ignoring me and he starts walking on his little doggie booboo.

"Toto, that's enough. Stop dragging your furry butt on the floor. I just got it waxed!" Mom yells, then starts pinning some burgundy velvet fabric on a dress form.

"These your friends from Kats and Kittys?" she asks.

"Yup."

"Where are you two from?" Mom asks, looking at Aqua.

Turning to look at me, then back to my mom, Aqua asks, "You mean me?"

Chanel kicks me. I kick her back.

"Yes, you, darling. You see anyone else here I don't know? You can call me Dorothea, by the way," Mom says.

"Oh, I'm sorry, Ms. Dorothea," Aqua says. "I didn't know you were talking to us. Um, we're from Houston."

"Houston. They have the best shopping mall in the world." Mom swoons. "And I should know. I've been to every shopping mall from here to Hong Kong. Did Galleria tell you I named her after the mall there?"

"The Galleria? Is that right?"

"That is right," Mom says, all pleased with herself. I've heard this story a ca-zillion times. "I was in Houston modeling for a fashion shoot. I was so bored because I didn't know anyone there—well, anyone I wanted to see— so I went shopping at the Galleria. That's where I bought my first pair of Gucci shoes," she goes on. "I was pregnant and I wanted to remember the moment forever. Most beautiful shoes I've ever had. Burgundy-sequined pumps with little bows in front."

"Kinda like Dorothy's ruby slippers?" Do' Re Mi asks, perking up.

"*Exactly.*" I smirk. "Mom still has the shoes in a leopard keepsake box, along with my baby pictures and a personal ad that she answered before I was born."

Now why did I say that? I have *such* a big mouth.

"Personal ad, what's that?" Do' Re Mi asks.

"It's for meeting people," Chuchie snips.

"You mean, like, for dating?" Angie asks.

"Yes. Like, for dating," Chuchie says with her *boca grande*.

"'Lonely oyster on a half shell seeks rare Black pearl to feel complete,'" Mom explains with a giggle.

"Galleria's mom answered the personal ad out of *New York Magazine*, and that's how she met her dad. Get it?" Chuchie explains some more. I am gonna get her later.

Aqua and Angie look at each other like they have just met the Addams family, then "chedda waves" catches herself and goes to pet Toto. "Wait until he meets Porgy and Bess," Angie coos, trying to pat his head, but he looks at her and yawns.

"Oh, how cute," Chanel says. "What kind of dogs are they?"

"Oh, they're not dogs," Angie chimes in.

"They're our guinea pigs from home. We couldn't leave them behind," Aqua explains, waiting to see my mom's reaction. I move my feet from Chanel quickly because I know she is going to kick me, but Aqua notices. "What's the matter?" Aqua asks me.

"Oh, nothing," I lie. "I thought I saw a roach."

"A roach!" My mom huffs. "There better not be any roaches in here or I'll go to that exterminator's office and exterminate him!"

"I was just joking, Mom," I say, quickly realizing that I don't want to endanger some poor man's life and leave his wife a widow. Mom would do it. Trust me.

"There's nothing wrong with guinea pigs for pets," Mom says, coming to Aqua and Angie's defense.

Why is she doing that, I wonder?

"Josephine Baker had a pet leopard. That's her," Mom says, pointing to the poster of Josephine. "She was the most famous Black singer and dancer in the world."

"She danced in banana skirts," Do' Re Mi says excitedly. "I know all about her. She was so famous, they shut down Paris just for her funeral."

"That's right, darling," Mom says, approving of Do' Re Mi. "Say, what are you divettes going to wear for the show?" Mom asks.

My mom knows full well the Whodunnit and the Whodini: 1. Why we are there. 2. How cheesy I will get to have her help us. 3. That I am desperate.

What she doesn't know is, I know how to turn the tables.

"Mom, you gotta give us some ideas!" I whine, even though it kills me. Mom loves to give "advice."

"Leopard is always the cat's meow, darling. How about some leopard cat suits? Then you can go to Fright Night on Prince Street and get some leopard masks with the whiskers, like you used to wear for Halloween when you were little. Some little leopard velvet boots or something, and the five of you would look fierce."

"I love it!" says Do' enthusiastically.

"That sounds fabbie poo, darling," I say, imitating my mother, then add for good measure, "Mom, can I get a weave for the show?"

"Do you have weave money?" Mom asks, then continues with her investigation before I get a chance to respond. "What are you going to call the group?"

"We haven't decided yet." I yawn, then pull out my Kitty Kat notebook, where I have written down a few names. "We thought of names like The Party Girls, The Ladybug Crew, A Taste of Toffee—that was Aqua's idea. The Ruby Slippers."

"Oooh, I like that," my mom says, smiling, then she hesitates. "But that's not for you girls."

"Why not?" Do' Re Mi asks.

"Darlings, I've been in this jungle a lot longer than you. Why don't you just stick with what you are instead of looking all over the place for answers?"

Mom then turns and looks at me. "The spots worked for Josephine Baker. They've worked for me. They'll work for you. Don't turn your back on your heritage."

"Your mom is funny," Aqua whispers in my ear. I can't believe it, but somehow the twins are getting along better with my mom than I am!

"'Member what that boy Derek called you in the hallway once?" Do' Re Mi asks me.

"What on earth did that Red Snapper say that was so deep?" I ask her.

"He called you a Cheetah Girl," Do' Re Mi says, then squeaks, "maybe we could all be the Cheetah Girls."

"Do' Re Mi, you are so on the money," Chuchie says, all excited.

"Yeah, we could be the Cheetah Girls," Aqua chimes in.

Angie claps her hands in delight.

Mom had been right. I was trying to be something I wasn't. I guess I can live with the Cheetah Girls, even though it wasn't my idea. Actually, I kinda like it!

"I love it!" Chuchie screams. We hug each other and scream so loud, my mom threatens to gag us and tie us up with fabric.

I catch Mom's eyes, then point to the backpacks, then to my friends, and mouth the word, "*Posso?*" which, in Italian, means "Can I, please?"

Mom doesn't even put up a fight. She walks over to the cheetah backpacks and gives one each to Do', Aqua, and Angie, like it was her idea. "Now, would you please settle down so I can take your measurements for the costumes," Mom says with a smile and a sigh.

"Omigod!" Do' Re Mi gasps, and runs over to give Mom a hug. There is something special between those two already. I'm glad.

Do' Re Mi turns to Angie and Aqua and says, "Y'all are okay with wearing cheetah cat suits, right?"

"That's right," Aqua says with a smile. "Dag. It's just a costume, Dorinda. We do have

Halloween in Texas, you know!"

"Hey, we gotta have a costume for Toto, too!" I say, in a sudden burst of inspiration. "He can be, like, our mascot!" This gets howls of approval, and an okay from my mom. Awright!

When we leave, Toto runs to the glass door and stares at us with his begging, beady eyes. We all wave at him. "Bye, Toto!" "Bye, boo-boo." "See you at show time, doggie-poo!"

Chapter 7

I need to resolve this music thing with Aqua and Angie, today. We have to begin practicing the songs I've written, now that we have the other two down.

Today, Dad drives me down to Chanel's house for rehearsal. He is late getting to the factory, so he is lost in his own world. "How are rehearsals going?" he asks me.

"Don't ask," I groan.

Dad wants me to be a singer, too. I think secretly that my singing has kept him and Mom together. Whenever they fight, I always start singing, and it makes them laugh.

"*Ciao*, Dad," I say, blowing him a kiss as I get out.

I'm glad that my parents are not coming to the bash. It's for Kats and Kittys only, thank gooseness. Between school, rehearsals, dance classes, and vocal classes, I am about to explode like microwave popcorn.

We have two hours to rehearse our vocals before we have to do our dance moves with Drinka.

"Listen, can we just do this?" I say to Aqua and Angie. I am holding my breath because I don't want to fight with them anymore.

Do' Re Mi is going along with the program. She kinda likes my songs. But the "Huggy Bear Twins" (me and Chuchie's secret nickname for them) are hard to please.

"All right," Aqua moans.

"We'll just start with the first verse today," I say, "so that Chuchie and Do' Re Mi can join in. You two listen up and try to come in where you know the words."

We start to sing:

"Some people walk with a panther
or strike a buffalo stance
that makes you wanna dance.

The Cheetah Girls

Other people flip the script
on the day of the jackal
that'll make you cackle.

But peeps like me
got the Cheetah Girl groove
that makes your body move
like wanna-be stars in the jiggy jungle.

The jiggy jiggy jungle!
The jiggy jiggy jungle!

So don't make me bungle
my chance to rise for the prize
and show you who we are
in the jiggy jiggy jungle!
The jiggy jiggy jungle!"

Why are Aqua and Angie leaning so heavy on the chorus? You can't even hear the rest of us! I wonder if they are doing it on purpose. Sure, they are better singers, but they don't have to sing like they're at the Thunderdome.

"Aqua, Angie, maybe you should sing the chorus a little softer so we can hear the harmony more?" I suggest.

"Oh, okay," they both say.

Chanel doesn't say anything. For someone who can run her mouth like she's doing a TV commercial on *Telemundo*, I can't get a squeak out of her when I need her to represent me. Why do I always have to stick up for us? And why is Do' Re Mi singing so softly?

"Do' Re Mi—you need to sing louder after the first verse, I think, no?"

"'But peeps like me got the Cheetah Girl groove,'" Do' Re Mi sings—this time with more gusto. "Like that?"

"Yeah," Aqua answers.

I'm wondering if anyone will boo at us at Kats and Kittys. Could they be that cold?

After dance rehearsal, we are standing outside of Drinka's building. By now, I've had about all I can take. Not only did the singing rehearsal go badly, but the dancing rehearsal went even worse. Especially Chanel—she was so busy giggling she couldn't even get through the numbers!

"Why don't you pay attention to what you're doing!" I scream at her now, losing my cool completely. Angie, Aqua, and Do' Re Mi get real quiet.

"What happened?" Chanel yells. "What did I do?"

"Chanel, you better not mess this up. You have to try to pay attention to what we're all doing so we look like we're doing the same moves."

"I'm not the one messing it up. You are, with your big mouth!" she screams at me. Chanel never screams. Only I do. We argue right there on the street.

Angie, Aqua, and Do' Re Mi wait on the sidewalk while me and Chanel are fighting. "I hate when you act so stupid and you don't listen to me!" I tell Chanel.

"You don't know what you're talking about, you chocolate-covered cannoli!"

No, she did not go there. So what if I was half Italian? She is Black and Latin. I never make fun of her. Well, almost never. I run all the way to the corner and put my arm up to get a taxi back home. It is my last ten dollars till Monday, but I don't care. I just want to run far away.

Do' Re Mi runs after me. "Y'all need to stop! Hold up, Galleria."

"No. I'm going home. I need to chill for now. I'm sorry, Do' Re, okay? I'll see you all tomorrow."

Once I am inside of my safe cheetah palace, I grab a box of my mom's Godiva chocolates. She keeps it hidden in the back of the kitchen cabinet. I don't care if she gets mad at me. So what? Everyone else is.

I take the Godiva box and get as far as I can under my blanket. I cry myself to sleep, slobbering on my leopard velvet pillow while I'm chomping on the candy. How could Chanel call me that? I feel like dragging her by her fake braids right down the street. I didn't even know she knew what a cannoli was.

I miss Toto. He's out at the dog groomer's—finally. Oh, well. He's probably just as glad I'm not suffocating him to death right now. Here I am, just fourteen years old, and my life is finished, I think, as I doze off into a deep sleep.

Chapter 8

What's harder than hiding a spotted cheetah in the desert? Trying not to speak to your best friend when the two of you go to the same school! By the time I left homeroom to make a mad dash to my color theory class, I was seeing spots from trying to keep my eyes glued on my desk so I would never look up and make eye contact with Chanel.

As I walked down the hallway, I concentrated on the answers for my quiz on primary colors: Red and yellow make orange. Blue and red make purple.

Hmmph, I hiss to myself. Chanel No. 5 can get on the stage by herself and eat Meow Mix for all I care.

"Galleria, Galleria!" Chanel yells, puffing down the hallway. She finally catches up to me, even though I still try to ignore her. "I just wanna know. You still want me to do your hair today after school?"

I am so mad, I forgot all about that. My mom is finally gonna let me get a weave, and Chanel is supposed to put it in.

"*Ciao-ciao*, chinchilla, cheetah," I snarl, shooing her away with my hand. "Pretend I'm not here. It's a mirage."

Breathing really hard, Chanel chokes on her words. "I had a bad dream last night, Galleria, for real. Please talk to me. *Per favore*, pleez."

Cheez whiz, Chanel No. 5 has finally learned something in her Italian class. I open my mouth to begin reading her the riot act when all of sudden I hear the word "Okay" slip out of my mouth.

"I dreamed we were on the stage, and you were screaming at me to dance faster, and I was so scared that I was gonna fall because the heels were so high on my shoes," Chanel says without breathing. "I tried to dance, but I fell so hard, and somehow—this is the weird part—I fell right into the people off the stage.

So I started screaming, right, and you, Do' Re Mi, Aqua, and Angie kept on singing. You acted like you didn't hear me scream. Then I tried to run because the people started chasing me and I just wanted to get away."

By now Chanel is giving tears for fears—real drama. So we hug. This was supposed to be fun for us, and it is turning into a *Nightmare on Broome Street*.

"My mom gave me fifty dollars for my weave. You think I could get two strands of hair for that?" I ask.

Chanel blinks at me. She can't believe I'm letting her off the hook this easy. I've got to admit, it's not like me. But I can't be mad at her. She's been my best friend forever, and I was acting kinda bossy and mean.

"Three at least!" she says, giggling. Then she gets serious. "I'm sorry for what I said," she confesses. "You made me mad. I didn't like what you said in front of Aqua that time."

"What time?" I ask.

"When we were at the Pizza Pit and you said I would be giving out *piñatas* later."

"Oh, I'm sorry," I tell her. "I was just playin'."

I was showing off in front of Aqua and

Angie. Now I see that Chanel did the same thing in front of them.

By the time school was out, we were rollin' like usual. First, we had to pick up leopard paper masks with gold whiskers from the Fright Night shop on Prince Street. Then we had to take the subway to Harlem to pick up Do' Re Mi at the YMCA, since she works so close to "It's Unbeweavable!," where they sell hair by the pound.

Do' Re Mi works at the Junior Youth Entrepreneurship Leadership Program Store in the Harlem YMCA. The program is designed for teens who need jobs and it's supposed to teach them leadership skills. Do' Re Mi had to complete a twelve-week curriculum on Saturdays, attend workshops during the week, and work in the store. I don't know how she does it all. She is yawning till the break of dawn half the time.

Because we never miss an opportunity to harmonize, and I am determined to get Do' Re Mi's voice at least a tidbit stronger in the soprano department, we start singing on Lenox Avenue as soon as we pick her up.

"Let's take it from the last verse," Chanel

says to Do' Re Mi, taking charge for a change.

"To all the competition, what can we say?
You better bounce y'all
'cause every Cheetah has got its day.

You better bounce y'all
'cause the Cheetah Girls are 'bout to pounce, y'all
and get busy in the jiggy jungle
no diggity, no doubt.

Get busy in the jiggy jungle.
The jiggy jiggy jungle.
The jiggy jiggy jungle.
The jiggy jiggy jungle!"

We are stylin' again—and more important, we are crew again—now and forever!

"I've never seen you with hair so long, Miss Thing," my mom says, touching my new Rapunzel weave. "But I still prefer to take my girls off at night and scratch my head."

Mom is, of course, referring to her wig collection. Angie and Aqua get a giggle out of this. They both have gotten their hair done—on the press and curl tip—and I think they're amused by my mom's wild and woolly wigs.

"Is it me, or is it hot in here? I'd better open the door and get some air in here." Mom doesn't wait for us to answer: she just opens the glass door and puts down the stopper hinge to stop the door from closing on its own. We are so excited because we are getting our final fitting for our cat suit costumes for the show tonight.

"Let me see your nails," Mom asks Aqua, who is definitely growing into the supa-show-off of the two. "What is that? Dollar bills?"

"Uh-huh," Angie answers proudly, flossin' about the gold dollar-bill sign decals she has put on her red tips.

"You trying to stay on the money, huh?" my mom says, smirking. "Well, you gotta make some first."

Angie and Aqua only get twenty-five dollars a week allowance apiece from their dad, but he also pays for them to get their nails done twice a month. I wonder if Angie spends as much time on her homework as she does on her nails.

"Fabbie poo," Chanel exclaims as she slips into her cat suit. "This is so phat!"

"Chuchie, you are gonna be over the leopard limit tonight, girlita!" My mom giggles.

The cat suits are all that. Each one has a mock turtleneck collar and zips up the back. Do' Re Mi's has a tail, too, because we thought that would be cute. Do' Re Mi puts on her cat suit, then flosses.

"You know how to work it, Miss Thing," Mom snips. "Not too tight?" Mom asks Do' Re Mi, who is prancing around like she's the cat's meow.

Do Re Mi's cat suit looks really tight, but when Mom asks her again, she just shakes her head sideways, smiling, and answers, "Cheetah *Señorita, está bien!*"

Mom smiles, then holds out a plate of Godiva chocolates for us to munch. She is being so nice to us. I poke Aqua, who excitedly takes a piece of chocolate and smiles. "Thank you, Mrs. Garibaldi. I mean, Miss Dorothea!"

Mom has told them more than once, "Call me Miss Dorothea, but just don't call me Heavy D!"

Aqua and Angie are so used to being formal around grown-ups, sometimes you can tell they don't know how to act normal.

I thought again about Chanel calling me a "chocolate-covered cannoli." I wouldn't tell Mom or she would make Chanel eat a whole box of them.

Chapter 9

The beauty mark Do' Re Mi paints right above her upper lip looks less fake than mine. I decided to try painting one smack dab in the middle of my cheek.

"She's a fake!" Do' Re Mi hums.

I rub off the cheesy dot of brown liquid liner and try it her way.

"Pa-dow! That's the dopiest dope one," Do' Re Mi says after I'm finished. She has dimples for days. I didn't think there was anyone cuter than Chuchie. I didn't think it was possible. But Do' is running a close second.

We have each painted on a beauty mark and put Glitterella sparkles around our eyes. Theme is everything, I keep repeating to myself. We are starting to be very meow-looking. (Even Aqua and Angie. It's amazing what a little makeup can do.)

"Harmony check!" yells Aqua.

"Welcome to the Glitterdome.
It's any place you call home.

Give me props, I'll give you cash,
then show you where my sparkles stashed.

Glitter, glitter. Don't be bitter!
Glitter, glitter. Don't be bitter!
Glitter, glitter. Don't be bitter!"

We were on point and almost finished "beating our faces," as Mom calls it. She says she thinks we may have a future. She came to one of the rehearsals at Chuchie's and watched.

"Dag on, Galleria. You should just give me this lipstick," Angie says, outlining her full smackers with my lipstick. Actually, we were splitting the one tube of S.N.A.P.S. lipstick in Flack between the five of us, but I was holding on to it.

"That's enough!" Chuchie yells. Flack is this metallic purple-blue color that may give mad effects under the Cheetah-Rama's strobe lights when we are onstage.

"It's not blue, Galleria. It looks more purple in the light,"Aqua says, holding up the tube.

"If you get hot sauce on it, it'll be red!" Chanel blurts out, then snatches Aqua's backpack. "Let me check your bag! You can't carry a bottle of hot sauce in your bag anymore. It could break and ruin everything. Just carry packets!" Do' Re Mi giggles.

"That's a Cheetah Girls rule!" I yell out. "Now, come on. We've got one hour to get to the club before show time."

"Do' Re Mi, you sure your cat suit isn't too tight?" Chanel asks, poking Do' Re Mi's butt and pulling her tail.

"No. I'm fine!" Do' Re Mi growls. "You think we'll be able to see onstage with these masks on?"

"We just ain't gonna move too close to the edge so we don't fall off!" says Angie.

Truth or dare be told, Angie and Aqua are lookin' more relaxed than the rest of us. They have more experience singing. And, besides, anyone who could get those church ladies to fall out in the aisles has serious skills. The only experience we had was talent shows and vocal lessons.

"Maybe we should just let Angie and Aqua sing for real, and we lip-synch into the mikes," I turn and say to Do' Re Mi and Chanel, 'cause I'm getting cold feet fast.

"Last dance. No chance," Do' Re Mi says, wiggling her matchstick butt.

We are gonna sing four songs—two of mine, and two of Kahlua's—"Don't Lox Me out the Box" and "The Toyz Is Mine." In the end, we decided to use tracks from all house music tapes to perform to, and sing the lyrics over them.

I can't believe this is happening. Not the performing part. I can believe that. Me and Chanel have been singing long enough into plastic hairbrushes to win the unofficial Wanna-be Stars in the Jiggy Jungle Award. I just can't believe we are actually going to make some money on the d.d.l. (the divette duckets license).

We walk over to the Cheetah-Rama in our outfits. "Cheetah Girls! Cheeetah Girls are in the house!" Chuchie yells down the block. It's Halloween, so everyone is looking at us and smiling.

We are only five blocks away from the Cheetah-Rama, which is at the end of West Broadway near the Mad Hatter Lounge. My mom goes there for tea on Sundays. The Cheetah-Rama is the dopiest dope club. They have cheetah couches and curtains, and my mom has been here a few times to dance because they play house music on special occasions. She drags Dad along, or sometimes Juanita, but sometimes she'll come by herself because she has a lot of old school friends who are still single and who still like to hang out.

This isn't the first time I've been in a nightclub, because last year we had the Kats and Kittys Klub Christmas Egg Nogger at the Hound Club in Harlem. But this is the first time I've hung out at a club that my mom the diva has danced at. I feel like it's the jointski, and I'm glad that no grown-ups are allowed here tonight—except for the Kats and Kittys Klub's staff and treasury committee.

Me and Chuchie have only been to the Cheetah-Rama in the daytime. It is kinda dark inside now, and I step on Aqua's foot because I don't see the decline of the ramp inside the entrance. I stumble for a few steps, and Chanel grabs my arm.

"Oh, snapples, Chuchie, 'member that dream you had? Well, it's not a dream!"

I don't care if I fall on my face. We've agreed to make our entrance wearing our masks, but my eyes haven't adjusted to the darkness.

You can tell it's Halloween, all right. The Cheetah-Rama is definitely haunted, with hundreds of Kats and Kittys wearing some pretty scary costumes.

"Hi, Mrs. Bugge," Do' Re Mi yells out. Her costume is hee-larious. She is wearing a green Afro, baseball uniform, and sneakers.

"Who is she supposed to be?" I ask, poking Aqua, who is staring at her.

"Menace Robbins!" she snips back.

"Oh, that guy from the Houston Oilys basketball team?" I ask.

"It's the Oilers!" Aqua snips.

Okay, so I never watch basketball games. Apparently, sports are a very big thing down south, according to the twins.

This is definitely a live party. It is wall-to-wall thumpin'—the music, the crowd, the lights. The excitement in the air is thumping, too.

The Cheetah Girls

People turn to look at us. The Cheetah Girls have definitely made an entrance. It was worth almost falling on my face!

"Cheetah Girls come out at night, baby!" I scream, throwing my hands in the air like I just don't care. Every eye in the house is on us, including some I can't see.

"Bubbles, don't look now," Chanel whispers. She is in back of me, pulling the tail on Do' Re Mi's cat suit, causing Do' to squeal. I turn, and Chanel whispers, "Don't look. Don't look."

I look, anyway. There is someone grinning in a Batman mask. "Holy, cannoli!" I giggle to Chanel. "Batman has big feet." Batman starts walking toward me, but his cape isn't flapping in the wind.

"Hey, Cheetah Girl!"

I know that voice. Oh, no, it can't be. The Red Snapper turned into a Caped Crusader? Gotham City is in deep herring. "Derek?"

"That's me. *C'est moi!*"

"Since when did you become a member?"

"Since you are, *ma chérie.*"

"Oh, it's like that," I say, smirking. His family has the duckets. Why am I surprised that he joined? Copycat.

"Are you taking French in school?" Chanel asks him, poking fun at him.

"*Oui, oui, mademoiselle,*" Derek says, grabbing Chanel's hand to kiss it.

"We're glad to see ya, Mr. *Oui, Oui!*" Chanel says, choking, taking her hand back and wiping it on her cat suit.

Derek seems so different without his Johnny BeDown hookups.

"Where's Robin?" I ask, referring to his friend Mackerel, who also goes to Fashion Industries High with us.

"He's not a Kats and Kittys member. He thinks it's mad corny."

"Too bad. You coulda been the dynamic duo."

"I got a Batmobile outside. Wanna ride later?"

"I don't know."

"Well, if you decide to, just give me the Batsignal." Derek laughs, pointing a flashlight in my face.

"*Au revoir*, Batman." Chanel says, wiggling her fingers.

"*Ciao*, Cheetah," he says to me. "Remember—you could be my Catwoman."

He does have good comeback lines, even if he was super-nervy right out of the box. Maybe Chanel is right—maybe I do think he's kinda cute, even if that gold tooth of his makes me laugh. *Not!*

Mrs. Bugge is signaling us to go backstage. It's show time. We run backstage and pick up the cordless mikes on the floor waiting for us. Then we line up five in a row behind the curtain, just like we rehearsed. Me and Chuchie are in the center. Do' Re Mi is standing to my left, and Aqua and Angie are together, next to Chanel.

"May the Force be with you," I tell Chuchie. This is something mystical, from a Star Wars movie, I think, but my mom always says it. I say it over and over again to myself.

Chuchie squeezes my hand. "Your hands are freezing, Bubbles," she whispers.

I almost wish Mom was here, because I am so scared.

I'm definitely on my own now. With my crew. Not in Mom's shadow. Me and Chuchie have followed the Yellow Brick Road just like we said we would. We made that promise to each other when we were seven years old. We would follow the Yellow Brick Road until we were independent and on our own—and, yes, had money of our own in our cheetah purses. We are never gonna work at Mikki D's.

"We'll always be crew. No matter what happens," I whisper to Chuchie, winking at her. I really do love Chuchie, my ace *señorita*. My fairy godsister.

Do' Re Mi is sniffling. "Do' Re, you're not crying, are you?" Chuchie asks her.

"No!" she giggles. I swear she cries more than the Tin Man. (I'm not supposed to know this, but Chuchie told me.)

My heart is pounding through my ears. At least I know I have one. Deejay Doggie Dawgs is lowering the music. That means it is definitely show time. No turning back.

"Are y'all ready, girls?" Mrs. Bugge asks, sticking her head behind the curtain.

"Ready for Freddy!" Aqua quips. "Freddy Krueger, that is."

Aqua loves her horror movies—and her horror-scope. I can't help but laugh. Freddy is probably out there. And Aqua probably invited him.

"Kats and Kittys. It's show time, and we have a very special treat for you tonight," Mrs.

Bugge announces to the crowd. "It's Halloween. How many of you are scared out there?"

The crowd boos. She is so corny.

"Well, I'll tell you the truth. I'm scared of the girls that I'm about to introduce you to. You may know them as Galleria Garibaldi, Chanel Simmons, Dorinda Rogers, and those singing twins from Houston, Aquanette and Anginette Walker, but tonight they are THE CHEETAH GIRLS, so give them a hand!"

I want to remember this night, forever. Absolutely forever. That is all I keep repeating to myself as the curtain goes up.

The strobe lights blind me in the face if I look too far back into the crowd. Now it is all about the beat. On three, we begin to sing, as if we've done this a hundred times—and the truth is, we have, in rehearsals.

"Don't lox me out the box, baby,
because you'll never know what side I'm buttered on.
My taste is sweet.
I can feel the heat . . ."

The Kats and Kittys are live. They are clapping along to Kahlua's song, and we are really getting into it. Everything is going just as we planned. They won't stop clapping. We wait before we go into the next song, and I try not to look into the audience. There are too many people, and I will lose my concentration.

It's time to sing "Welcome to the Glitterdome." On this song, we are facing the curtain, then we are supposed to turn to sing from the side profile as the strobe lights flash on and off to imitate stars in the sky.

Even out of the corner of my eye I can see that Angie and Aqua are still seconds off from the dance cues. They don't turn as fast as the rest of us do! I do not let this distract me, but I pray that no one notices.

Oh, I could just die, I'm thinking, when it's Do' Re Mi's turn to take center stage and do her split. This is when I see people I know smiling at me. Kats and Kittys who live in Manhattan. They are all in the house!

I am smiling from ear to ear, then pouting on cue as the song goes along. My mike is going in and out, but I can hear a sound as distinct as the sweetest melody—it is the sound of Do' Re

Mi's cat suit splitting. A sound I will never forget! She is giggling, and so is everyone else. The people closest to the stage are pointing and giggling at her. They not only heard it, but they saw it happen, too!

Bless her little heart, as Aqua would say. Do' Re Mi keeps dancing, she doesn't stop, but she cannot do the somersault at the top of "Wannabe Stars in the Jiggy Jungle" or everyone would see the split in her cat suit—and her leopard underpanties. "Go Cheetah Girls! Go Cheetah Girls!" the crowd is chanting.

By this point, me and Chuchie are laughing, but the show must go on. Everyone is clapping at us, and it doesn't matter that Do' Re Mi's cat suit is split, or that Aqua and Angie don't turn on the right cue. We did it! We did it!

The clapping doesn't stop. "Wanna-be Stars in the Jiggy Jungle" is the song the audience loves best. We can tell by how hard they clap at the end. We take our bows, and lift our masks off, and throw kisses, just like we planned.

When the curtain comes down, we scream. "Oh, my gooseness, lickety splits!" Chanel shouts, grabbing Do' Re Mi's booty as we scramble into the dressing room. "That's what you get for showing off!"

When we get into the dressing room, Do' Re Mi chews out Aqua and Angie. "Aqua, Angie, you two gotta turn faster when we do that pivot step. What were y'all thinking about?" Do' Re Mi gets all bossy as she changes into her velvet leopard leggings. We stay in our costumes as planned and take our masks off. I'm sweating like crazy.

"We about to get paid, baby," Chuchie yells.

"We don't get our money till next week," I call out.

Chanel sighs. "I know. I'm just sayin'."

There is a knock on the door. "Go away. We're not ready to come out!" I shout.

Mrs. Bugge sticks her head in the doorway anyway. "There is someone who wants to see you girls, so hurry on out."

"It's probably Batman!" Chanel quips.

"No, it's the Joker." Do' Re Mi clowns, and spreads her lips.

"It's the Penguin!" I snap. "And he wants to dance with me." We all squeal and laugh.

"Seriously, though," I finally say, "we're gonna need more practice."

"Yeah," says Do' Re Mi. "And I'm gonna

need a bigger costume."

"Oh, snapples!" Chanel giggles.

"You should have told my mom," I say, trying to be nice to Do' Re Mi, because I know she must feel bad. "She would have made you a bigger one."

"I didn't want to say anything," Do' Re Mi says softly.

"Why not?" I ask.

"You don't understand," she says, blinking back tears. "You'll never know what it's like to have to take everything that people give you just because you're a foster child. Nobody ever made me anything before. I didn't think I deserved it, and I didn't want to screw it up. I'm sorry," she whispers.

"That's okay, baby. Next time, you better open up that little mouth of yours and speak up!" Angie says.

There will be a next time—that's for sure.

"We still coulda served seconds. They were loving us!" Aqua says, lapping up the victory. "Now everybody knows the Cheetah Girls are ready to pounce."

"*You* are, that's for sure," Chanel says, smirking.

Then I say what I cannot believe, but know to be true. "I want us to stay as a group, no matter what happens. Even if we don't make any money."

"Oh, I'm definitely buying a ranch back home," Angie says, snarling. "I don't know about y'all."

"You know what I'm saying."

"We know what you're saying," Do' Re Mi says sweetly.

I spread out my hands so we can form a call-of-the-wild circle. "Let's take a Cheetah Girls oath."

I make up the oath right on the spot.

"We're the Cheetah Girls and we number five.
What we do is more than live.
We'll stay together through the thin and thick.
Whoever tries to leave, gets hit with a chopstick!
Whatever makes us clever—forever!!!"

Then we do the Cheetah Girls hand signal. Stretching out our hands, we touch each other's fingertips, wiggling them against each other.

"None of us ain't ever gonna drop out of the

group, like Rosemary from The Spice Rack Girls, right?" Aqua jokes.

"*Riiight*," Do' Re Mi says with a drawl.

"And none of us are gonna burn down our boyfriends' houses if we get famous, *riiiight?*" Chuchie yells out.

"*Riiiiight*," we all chime in as we head out of our matchbox dressing room to get our groove on.

The music and screams are loud. Really loud. Mrs. Bugge is standing in the hallway with a tall man wearing a yellow tie and a red suit. I don't think it's a costume. But you never know.

"Girls, someone wants to meet you. He's a manager, and a business associate of Mr. Hare, the owner of the club. Mr. Johnson, I want you to meet the Cheetah Girls."

"How you doin'? I'm Aquanette and this is my sister, Anginette. Did you see us perform?"

I clear my throat so I can talk. "Hi, I'm Galleria, and this is Chanel and Dorinda," I say to Mr. Johnson. I wonder what he thought of our performance.

"Nice to meet you," Mr. Johnson says, shaking my hand. "Well, you girls are cute. I came down to pick up a check from Mr. Hare, and I thought I would stick around and check out your act."

Our act. That sounds pretty cool.

"I heard the name of the group—the Cheetah Girls, and it sounded cute. I was wrong, though," Mr. Johnson continues.

"What do you mean?" I ask him, feeling my cheeks turn red.

"You were splendiferous. Fantastic. Marvelistic. You know what I mean?" Mr. Johnson says.

He sure has a way with words. We all laugh and get excited. A manager! I wonder what that is.

"What do you do?" I ask him.

"Oh, I'm sorry. My name is Jackal Johnson, and I have a company called Jackal Management Group. I think you girls need a good manager like me to get you a record deal. You understand?"

"We understand," Do' Re Mi chimes in.

"Here is my card. I'll expect to hear from you soon. I think, with the right management and direction, the Cheetah Girls can really go places—and I'd like to take you there. We can set up a meeting for next week."

"We'll call you," Chanel says, holding my arm.

"Next week," I add.

When we head down to the party, it's like a dream. Just the way I've imagined it a thousand times. Now it's really happening!

"I have one thing to say," says Do' Re Mi, sashaying to the dance floor. "The Spice Rack Girls had better bounce, baby, 'cause the Cheetah Girls are 'bout to pounce!"

No diggity, no doubt!

"Wanna-be Stars in the Jiggy Jungle"

Some people walk with a panther
or strike a buffalo stance
that makes you wanna dance.

Other people flip the script
on the day of the jackal
that'll make you cackle.

But peeps like me
got the Cheetah Girl groove
that makes your body move
like wanna-be stars in the jiggy jungle.

The jiggy jiggy jungle!
The jiggy jiggy jungle!

So don't make me bungle
my chance to rise for the prize
and show you who we are
in the jiggy jiggy jungle!
The jiggy jiggy jungle!

Some people move like snakes in the grass
or gorillas in the mist
who wanna get dissed.

Some people dance with the wolves
or trot with the fox
right out of the box.

But peeps like me
got the Cheetah Girl groove
that makes your body move
like wanna-be stars in the jiggy jungle.

The jiggy jiggy jungle!
The jiggy jiggy jungle!

So don't make me bungle
my chance to rise for the prize
and show you who we are
in the jiggy jiggy jungle!
The jiggy jiggy jungle!

Some people lounge with the Lion King
or hunt like a hyena
because they're large and in charge.

Some people hop to it like a hare
because they wanna get snared
or bite like baboons and jump too soon.

But peeps like me
got the Cheetah Girl groove
that makes your body move
like wanna-be stars in the jiggy jungle.

The jiggy jiggy jungle.
The jiggy jiggy jungle.

So don't make me bungle
my chance to rise for the prize
and show you who we are
in the jiggy jiggy jungle!

The jiggy jiggy jungle.
The jiggy jiggy jungle.

Some people float like a butterfly
or sting like a bee
'cause they wanna be like posse.

Some people act tough like a tiger

to scare away the lynx
but all they do is double jinx.

But peeps like me
got the Cheetah Girl groove
that makes your body move
like wanna-be stars in the jiggy jungle.

The jiggy jiggy jungle.
The jiggy jiggy jungle.

So don't make me bungle
my chance to rise to the prize
and show you who we are
in the jiggy jiggy jungle.

The jiggy jiggy jungle!
The jiggy jiggy jungle!

The Cheetah Girls Glossary

bank: Money, loot.

boho: An artsy-fartsy black bohemian type.

bomb: Cool.

bozo: A boy who thinks he's all that, but he's really wack.

cheese for it: Manipulate.

cheez whiz: Gee whiz.

chomp-a-roni: Trying to catch a nibble on the sneak tip.

cuckoo for Cocoa Puffs: Going bonkers.

diva size: Dress size fourteen and up.

divette-in-training: A girl who can't afford Prada or Gucci—yet.

don't be bitter!: Go for yours!

duckets: Money, loot.

flossin': Showing off.

goospitating: Looking at someone cute like they're lunch.

growl power: The brains, heart, and courage that every true Cheetah Girl possesses.

jiggy jungle: A magical place inside of every big city where dreams really come true—and every cheetah has its day!

majordomo dope: Legitimate talent.

nosy posy: A person who is nosy and can't help it.

one up, two down: One-upmanship.

pastamuffin: A dog with wiggly hair.

peeps: People.

powder to the people!: Never leave home without your compact.

raggely: In need of beauty parlor assistance.

smirfs: Smirks.

wack-a-doodle-do: Very corny.

wanna-be: Not a real player—yet!

ABOUT THE AUTHOR

Deborah Gregory earned her growl power as a diva-about-town contributing writer for ESSENCE, VIBE, and MORE magazines. She has showed her spots on several talk shows including OPRAH, RICKI LAKE, and MAURY POVICH. She lives in New York City with her pooch, Cappuccino, who is featured as the Cheetah Girls' mascot, Toto.

 JUMP AT THE SUN